Praise for BODY

Wry, heartwarming, and richly dramatic, these stories reach across decades, from troubled young adulthood to precarious old age, and reaffirm what remains human and vulnerable in all of us.

TARA ISON, author of *Reeling Through Life* and *Child Out of Alcatraz*

MacDonald's immersive language makes us inhabit the bodies of her vividly drawn characters through sensations: the chill of a dark, empty church at night; the softness of an old woman's skin; or the warm and soothing taste of chocolate. These are sensations that reveal what runs beneath the physical—the soul's yearning to connect with our fellow humans. MacDonald's profound insight and her compassion are triumphs of this indelible collection.

LYNN SLOAN, author of *This Far Isn't Far Enough* and *Principles of Navigation*

MacDonald reads the room in each story and sees not just the postures and worn shoes of their inhabitants, but also their inner states. Throughout this collection, she builds many such rooms for her readers to survey, populated by people whose body language speaks volumes. The fictional worlds are fully fleshed-out, and the stories' wide-ranging premises and subtle endings yield a sense of wonder...A well-wrought collection that finds moments of transcendence in the personal quests of its characters.

KIRKUS REVIEWS

...a literary, psychologically engrossing series of portraits of individuals who, in different ways, stand at the crossroads of change...

DIANE DONOVAN, for *Midwest Book Review*

MacDonald's savvy understanding of human relationships and her lucid, rugged, and vibrantly poetic prose, make for riveting stories you can't put down and must pause at length between, imagining what came before and what comes next.

RICHARD LEMM, author of *Shape of Things to Come* and *Burning House*

...unforgettable portraits of people crossing out of hopeless suspension into vulnerable hope and tender communion.

KEVIN MCILVOY, author of *Little Peg* and *The Fifth Station*

Some characters come into our lives and are forgotten after the turn of the last page. The characters in Marylee MacDonald's short story collection, *Body Language*, aren't just coming over for dinner. Her characters become instant grandmothers, sisters, troubled cousins, and departed loved ones. Each story drives the nails of connection and bonds down deeper. The writing style itself is smart but relaxed, and the story unfolds easily in your mind . . . The stories are so vastly different on some levels, and on others they reflect the same message. We are human, we all feel love, fear, sadness, and bitterness, and no one can escape these, no matter how hard we try not to step into that bear trap of pathos. It is my fervent belief that anyone who reads this book may possibly be healed of some sort of trauma. I know that it helped me deal with some of my own familial problems. Any book that can release even a molecule of emotion that sadly has nowhere to go but within is a book that needs to be read and passed on by word of mouth.

ERIN NICHOL COCHRAN, for *Readers' Favorites*

Body Language

Short Stories

Twelve unforgettable portraits of heartbreak and desire

Body Language

Short Stories

Twelve unforgettable portraits of heartbreak and desire

MARYLEE MACDONALD

Grand Canyon Press

www.grandcanyonpress.com

Publisher's Cataloging-in-Publication Data
MacDonald, Marylee
Body language : short stories / Marylee MacDonald.
217 pages ; cm

ISBN: 978-1-951479-95-4 (paperback) | 978-1-951479-00-8 (Kindle) | 978-1-951479-01-5 (epub) | 978-1-951479-02-2 (pdf) | 978-1-951479-03-9 (audiofile)

LCSH: Aging — Fiction. | Aging – Psychological aspects – Fiction. | Fertility –

Fiction. | Substance abuse – Fiction. | Mothers and daughters – Fiction. | Mothers and sons – Fiction. | Touch – Psychological aspects – Fiction. | Interpersonal relations – Fiction. | Bildungsromans. | LCGFT: Short stories.

LCC: PS3613.A2714255 B63 2020 | DDC: 813/.6--dc23

"A Body of Water," first published as "Evolution Valley" in *The Mountain Pass: A Zimbell House Anthology*; "All I Have," first published in *Seven Hills Literary Review*: 2020; "The Memory Palace," first published in *The Sandy River Review*; "Voices," first published in *CALYX* as "Falling in Flight"; "The Blue Caboose," first published in the *Willisden Herald: New Short Stories #11* as "Caboose"; "Tito's Descent," first published in *The Writing Disorder*, 2019-2020.

Printed in the United States of America

Cover design by: www.tatlin.net

Body Language is a work of fiction. Names, characters, places, and incidents either are the product of the author's imagination or are used fictitiously. Any resemblance to actual persons, living or dead, events, or locales is entirely coincidental.

1 2 3 4 5 6 7 8 9 10

For Bruce

I have perceiv'd that to be with those I like is enough,

To stop in company with the rest at evening is enough,

To be surrounded by beautiful, curious, breathing, laughing flesh is enough,

To pass among them or touch any one, or rest my arm ever so lightly round his or her neck for a moment, what is this then?

I do not ask any more delight, I swim in it as in a sea.

From "The Body Electric" by
WALT WHITMAN

PREFACE

———○———

THE STORIES IN this book are about people who follow their instincts. Their bodies, rather than their conscious minds, direct what they do.

A few years back, I became interested in the neuroscience of
human behavior and discovered that many of our actions, if not
most, originate in the amygdala, the primitive brain that is the
site of our "flight or fight" response. Our five senses collect data
from our surroundings, and that data is instantly transformed
into electrical signals. These signals travel up the spinal cord to
the amygdala, the hunter-gatherer's primitive brain.

The amygdala is hard-wired to the cortex, the part of the
brain that makes instant judgments. Is that stranger friend or
foe? Is that relative the same uncaring bastard we've always
thought he or she was, or can we let down our guard and finally
resolve the childhood hurts that shaped who we've become?
Without the intervention of conscious thought, our bodies
make instantaneous decisions about whether we're safe or in
danger.

What's even more fascinating is that there's often a time lag
between our actions and words. We've raised our fists or run for

cover before we have time to think, "Gosh, I'd better book it!" That's why we wake up in the middle of the night, pondering the "could have saids" and "should have saids." There's a delay between the instant our bodies *feel* an emotion and the moment we *find the perfect words* to *name* our feelings.

Attraction works much the same way. When we're attracted to someone, the hormones dopamine and norepinephrine pump into the bloodstream. The hormonal cocktail makes us feel positively giddy. Even relatively innocent contact, such as hugging, increases the "love" hormone: oxytocin. Maybe that's why Walt Whitman, in his poem "The Body Electric," says he is content to swim in the sea of touch.

The following passage from the story, "Tito's Descent," sums up the theme of the collection.

"I had never been as aware of my body as I was at that moment. The warmth of another human being, the sideways pressure of his hip, the squeeze of his fingers against my arm, the ripple of sensation from my forehead to my feet, made me feel as if we humans were designed, on a primitive level, to connect with one another not just with words, but with the intimacy of touch; that touch was essential for our well-being and the reason we have bodies, not just souls."

Our bodies speak to us every day.

Let us listen.

Marylee MacDonald
Santa Rosa, California
January, 2020

TABLE OF CONTENTS

A BODY OF WATER

―――――○―――――

THE FIRST TIME I saw Sally, she was leaping from the top rail of a corral fence and into the saddle of one of her daddy's prized stallions, Satan.

At thirteen I was tall for my age (I'd try out for the freshman basketball team in the fall but would make junior varsity instead). Even so, the magnificent horse stood hands above me. Sally's guts and grace stopped me in my tracks. Seeing her all-American good looks, my knees began to cave.

Sally's dad owned Muir Trail Ranch up near Florence Lake, a deal he'd worked out with the Forest Service and that gave him the right to run trail rides. He had taken me on as a part-time ranch hand, and by the summer after senior year, I was a full-fledged groom.

I thought the summer would give me a chance to spend more time with Sally, edge aside the guy she'd been going with. But one hot day in August, when I had just turned eighteen, Sally married him, and so it was me who stood in polished boots and a dress-white shirt, shooing away a misery of mosquitoes with my Stetson and awaiting the new bride's arrival back at the ranch. Without making eye contact, I held the reins while Sally, in a wedding dress and cowboy boots, dismounted.

She headed off to supervise the barbecue and greet her guests. While brushing down Satan in his stall, I let it go. Cracking the knuckles of my freaky long fingers, I let it all go. That seals it, I thought. She made her choice. The next day I enlisted in the Navy.

When I got back my dad helped me buy a ranch near Sumner Hill, but a ranch in the foothills didn't sit right. I bought another higher up, edging my way back to the place I'd been happiest in my life. Once or twice a year my wife let me off the leash, and I packed up my fishing pole and headed up State Route 168. When that first sweet smell of Ponderosa pine came through the open windows, my heart began to pound.

Twenty years had gone by since Sally's wedding, six years since my own, and in the ensuing years, I had forced myself into some kind of normal life. If I saw Sally at all, it was when she was tying horses to the hitching post and waiting for the day's trail riders to finish their steak and eggs. Occasionally, we would bump into each other at the hot springs out behind the ranch. Once, we happened to be sitting in the steaming water when the sky opened up in a typical Sierra thunderstorm: brief and unannounced. The privacy afforded by pebbles of rain socking against the canvas lean-to above our heads was an open invite to laugh and tell stories about kids we'd gone to high school with or guys like me who'd worked summers riding trail or washing dishes. Being friends with Sally wasn't quite like being friends with another guy, but out of respect for her husband, I pretended it was and never made my move.

Anyway, early last spring before my last son was born, who should I see driving up to my front door but Sally. She parked her yellow pick-up by the stoop and walked up, snugging her tan riding pants around her hips. Over the winter, she'd put on a few pounds, but summer always slimmed her down.

"Hey, there." I greeted her with an open door. "What brings

you down this way?"

"Well, I don't know exactly why I came, John." She undid her ponytail, then spitting on her fingers, cinched it up again. The worry lines on her forehead matched the squint lines around her eyes. We were both getting older.

"Come on in and meet the kids," I said, taking her elbow.

"I won't take but a minute," she said.

"You're not interrupting anything."

Seven months pregnant, short and stocky, Margie waddled out of the kitchen. With her curly brown hair and apron tied up under her breasts, she looked a little unnerved by Sally turning up like this. Margie wiped her hand, front and back, as she'd been flouring chicken, then offered a handshake. Over the years Margie had heard me mention Sally, mostly in connection with my summers as a young, single ranch hand. However, actually seeing Sally, with her square jaw and athletic build, her 5′11″ frame, and her horse-riders' bowlegs, well, that was a whole different deal.

"You want to meet my kids?" I asked.

"I'll go see what they're up to," Margie said, not taking her eyes off Sally.

"I can go out back if that's where they are," Sally said.

"No, I'll get them." Margie slammed the patio door.

The hallway where we stood was a regular rogue's gallery of family pictures.

Sally leaned in for a better look. "Cute kids."

"Let me show you around the Ponderosa," I said and apologized for the dirt on my hands. "I was putting in some walnuts."

"Can't stay long. Just wanted to know if you'd like to go fishing up by Colby Meadow."

"It's early."

"I think we could get up that far."

"Horses or foot?"

"It'll have to be on foot. I don't want to take the animals. Water's too high."

"I guess I could do that."

Out back, through the closed door, I could hear Margie doing the two-tone call. "Jaaas-son! Raaan-dy! You boys get in here right now, and don't make me come find you." She would be back any minute.

"When you want to do this?" I said, lowering my voice.

"A week from today."

"How about in two weeks."

"No, a week," she said. "Has to be."

"I guess that can be arranged."

Sally seemed anxious to leave, and I walked her to the truck. Margie brought the kids around to the driveway. Jason was going on six and Randy five. Sally looked at me. She probably hadn't bothered to figure out the math, and I had never told her I'd had to get married. Either that or she just figured my kids weren't real, like the characters in a movie everyone else is talking about but you haven't yet seen. She pulled a handkerchief out of her pocket and wiped Randy's nose. She asked him what he'd been doing, and when he pulled out a blue belly lizard, she took it and stroked its chin. Randy's eyes got wide. His mom never let him bring lizards in the house. In fact, if anything, Margie was a little at odds with the natural world. She'd grown up in Sacramento.

Sally handed back the lizard and told the boys she hoped I would bring them up to the ranch sometime. She shook hands with Margie again, Margie gave me a look, and then of all things, Sally took my hand, letting her own go limp.

I wanted to ask her what the heck this handshake business was all about and why she avoided looking me in the eye, but before I could get the words out, she turned her back and strode resolutely toward her truck, as if we'd agreed on a loan. Sally got in, threw an arm across the seat, and backed one-handed out to the road.

Puzzled, I watched from the porch and felt my stomach turning the way it does when I'm coming down with the flu. I was not quite sure if I should go to bed or stand my ground and hope it passed. Margie slid past me. "You going to stand out here all night?"

"Is dinner ready?"

"Soon as you set the table," she said, "and I don't mean set *at* the table."

ALL WEEK I worked like the devil to get the walnuts in and adjust the irrigation. When Margie heard me going through my tackle box, she came out to the garage. Splay-footed, she stood massaging her stomach. We had sort of joked about "accidents," how they happened, why we'd been careless, how I should have pulled out and let her put more jelly in her diaphragm.

"What if the baby comes early?" she asked.

"That's why I'm going now," I said, bending over my pack so she didn't see my face, which would have told her I was lying. "In another month I wouldn't risk it."

"Get it out of your system, then." She slammed the door, her signal that she'd be stewing about it for some while.

It had taken a day or two of deep thinking to figure out what Sally was up to. I have not been entirely faithful to my wife, and from the tone of Sally's voice — and even more from her limp hand; so unlike her usual crush-your-fingers-to-prove-a-point grip — I guessed she wanted me to sleep with her, but I didn't know why. There are certain conditions where I wouldn't sleep with a woman, one of them being if she was mad at her man, and I was just convenient revenge. Her man or her father, in Sally's case, because her father was the domineering type. And the other case was where some gal wanted to get me tangled into the web of her life. I already made that mistake with Margie. Turned out she wasn't a bad wife, as wives go.

But as I was driving up to Florence Lake, singing and whistling my way around the curves, it struck me that in spite of my financial security and the enjoyment I took in my kids, this truly happy feeling came over me less often than when I was young.

I parked my truck down the road from the boat dock, shut up the cab, and threw the keys under the left front wheel, since one year I'd lost the keys in a stream and had to hitch a ride home to get the spare. Besides, when you're going into the back country, it's freeing to leave all but what you absolutely need behind.

The outboard that carried people from the dock over to Sally's father's ranch was out on the lake, and I thought about waiting till it came back. That would cut three miles off however long I had to hike today. Then it occurred to me that maybe Sally didn't want my presence to be public knowledge. I could walk the three miles in less than an hour, and so I did.

I was all the way around the lake and heading up the granite ridge toward the ranch when I saw Sally heading toward me. She was concentrating on the trail, looking down at the rocks and taking the slope in giant strides. She had on a sheepskin coat with her thumbs tucked in the pockets. Her long brown hair was clipped at the back of the neck, and her eyes shown as blue-green as the lake. When she smiled, it wasn't seductive, but rather open, frank, and warm. Just the same, I felt a jump in my groin.

"Hey, Sally!" I shouted.

"Shh!" She put her finger to her lips. "Do you need a hand with your gear?"

I climbed to where she was waiting on a boulder. "What's the deal?"

"Come on. Let's go up this ridge and cut over to Blayney Meadow. I left my pack there. Did you bring flies? I didn't have time to tie any."

"I've got buzz hackles."

"They think I'm just going up by myself. My husband wanted to come, but I'm trying to think a little, and I can't when he's around."

"But you can with me? Why didn't you go alone? You're not about to get lost."

"I wanted company. Come on. We've got four days to talk." She pushed me ahead. Like me, Sally must have made her excuses. I wondered what she'd brought to eat. Cornbread, I hoped. That went well with fish. But if she just grabbed food from the storeroom, we'd be cooking freeze-dried turkey tetrazzini. The smell of frying bacon drifted over from the ranch and made my mouth water.

"That there bacon smells good," I said. "I haven't had bacon in forever."

"Cholesterol?" Sally said.

"Yep. Getting old."

Sally smiled and grabbed her pack from a tree. "You've still got a little life in you, I reckon."

"Hope so," I said. "Be a shame to check out early."

We went up the trail, stepping around mule deer pellets, and walked in silence until lunch, when we stretched out on the ground, resting our heads on our packs. Most women talked your ear off. Sally was the exception. Offering her a handful of trail mix, I must have been watching her out of the corner of my eye.

"Stop staring," she said. "I'm not that fascinating." She scrambled to her feet and walked over to the river, dipping her Sierra cup.

I retied my boots. If she wanted to be like that, I wouldn't look at her again ever, and she could see how she liked being ignored. She drank her fill, then refilled the cup and brought me my first taste of sweet, pure — almost thick — mountain water.

My jaw unclenched. Look out, John, I thought. This woman is a peck of trouble.

"Want a hand up?" she asked.

"I was just enjoying the sound of the river," I said, "but I guess you want to go."

"I do," she said.

THE TRAIL GREW slick. An open bog smelled like a dead marmot. Skunk cabbage. Further on, snow flowers, like stalks of red asparagus, poked through the duff of fallen needles. It was early yet for Indian paintbrush and penstemon; but, there was plenty of lupine, a good sign because it meant we likely wouldn't get snowed on.

By the time we came upon a campsite, the sun had dropped behind the trees. "Let's stop here," I said.

She pulled out a topo map and spread it on a log. "Before it gets too dark, we should talk about our final destination."

I bent over the map. Her hair brushed my cheek. The creamy vanilla scent of frozen custard. She'd been smelling like that since high school, and I almost licked her neck.

Seemingly unaware of my rapid breathing, she put her finger on a small lake. "Let's go here!"

"Sure." She knew the good places to camp. "We going to cook on propane?" I said.

"Nope. I have a fire permit."

This early in the season, the ground was saturated, and even if a spark hit the duff, pine needles wouldn't burn. By the time I came back with downed wood, Sally had made a cook-fire from twigs. A pot of coffee balanced on a rock. While she boiled water, I rolled out our sleeping bags and put them a foot apart.

"Is that okay with you?" I asked. "Or you want the fire between us?"

"What, like cowboys in movies?" She was squatting over the fire, pouring out a silver pack of dehydrated spaghetti. "No, John, I'll bed down next to you." She gave me a thumbs up.

After we'd eaten and washed dishes, we sat across from one other on logs. I sang Garth Brooks' songs. She liked my voice, even when it got choked up from thinking of the three summers at the ranch, back when we were kids, and how she'd never given me the time of day. 'Course, she was a year older and that made all the difference at that age. I put on another pot of coffee. Caffeine might keep me awake, but it didn't matter. I was too keyed up to sleep.

I kept waiting for Sally to tell me why she'd invited me on this trip, but all she talked about was the tourists at the ranch. A lot of the old regulars, people who'd watched her grow up, were getting on in years, and now their kids and grandkids were coming up.

"What do you think about when you're alone, John?" She had her arms wrapped around her knees and held a coffee cup tight in one hand.

I tried to see her face. I could usually tell more about what she was thinking by how she looked, in spite of the way she tried not to let her feelings come out that way either.

"I guess I'm not alone that much," I said.

"I'm always alone." She stretched her feet out to the fire and tapped the toes of her boots. Then she yawned.

A signal. That part of the talk was over. In the flickering light I caught her looking at me quickly, maybe to see if I would take the bait. People with a mind to fool around always make out that their spouse is the Devil incarnate.

"I have to apologize about this body." I stood, patted my belly, and kicked dirt on the fire. "I'm a little out of shape."

She looked me up and down. "Could have fooled me."

I laughed.

"Leave a few coals for morning," she said. "It's easier to start."

I stopped kicking. Out of the corner of my eye, I watched Sally walk over to our sleeping bags, strip down to her underwear, and crawl into her blue cocoon. Didn't look like she had in mind what I thought she did.

"Damn," I said, digging through my pack. "I forgot my long johns."

"Just sleep in your birthday suit."

"I don't favor waking up at night and having to stand buck-naked while I take a leak."

"You're right," she said. "Another hour, and it'll drop below freezing."

I kept on my flannel shirt and folded my jeans for a pillow. When my bag was zipped, I put my hand on her shoulder. "You still awake?"

"I'm looking at the stars," she said.

They made us learn our stars in the Navy. I guess they thought if we were ever stranded on a desert island, we could get home. Above, where the treetops almost joined, I could see Orion.

"Do you know the constellations?" I said.

"My father made me learn them."

"Your father kind of overprepared you for life."

"What kind of thing is that to say?"

"I don't know. It was more a feeling than anything. How you had to be the best at tracking. The best female barrel racer. What you didn't get any encouragement for was just being yourself. Did you ever even wear makeup?"

I waited, but she didn't say anything.

"Good night, Sally," I said after a while.

"Good night, John," she answered.

"We sound like the Waltons."

"I always wanted a big family," she said. "That's coming from me, by the way. Not my dad."

THE NEXT DAY I got up early, started the fire, and made coffee. Sally hardly touched her breakfast. She didn't like to hike on a full stomach. After a couple hours walking, a stop for lunch, and another hour on the trail, we bushwhacked to the little lake. Since it was a pretty easy day, we got out her pole and I dug out my flies. While we waited for the fish to rise, I showed her how I tied a buzz hackle, and she showed me a woolly worm that she thought worked pretty well in spring runoff. About the time we cast our flies, the wind died down. We ate the fish and boiled up some RiceARoni, but between the mosquitoes and Cutter's spray stinging our eyes, we had a miserable dinner and climbed into our bags, holding them closed at the top and nearly suffocating.

I woke before sunup and got breakfast over quick so we could skedaddle before getting attacked. Since all the lower lakes were sure to have mosquitoes if this one did, we decided to head up to Evolution Valley. The only problem with the plan was that no one had been up there yet, and the snow had been heavy.

WE RETRACED OUR steps back to the place we'd camped the night before. Just beyond that campsite, after we had crossed a slick, striped granite saddle, we ran into our first patches of snow. Switchbacking steadily uphill, my boots left pink sink-holes. Then we walked for what felt like a long, long ways before I noticed that the lodgepoles, junipers, and aspen grew closer together and that the ground had leveled out. Fallen wood and crusted snow made it hard to see the trail. Sally led, going by the diagonal slash marks on the trees.

Back in high school a Forest Service crew had taken me along as a mule wrangler when they went to blaze the trail. Twenty odd years ago the ax marks had left gashes on the trunks and sap oozing like tears. I hadn't been up this way since. The bark had regrown, filling in like scar tissue around a wound, but seeing those slashes made me miss that mule. My shoulders ached from the weight of my pack, and I stopped to adjust the straps.

When I caught up to Sally, she was standing at the edge of a vast tangle of branches. Trees lay on their sides, their tops pointing downhill. An avalanche.

"This is going to be a bear," she said.

"Do you want to head back?" I asked.

"No, we can make it." She began picking her way. The tree trunks were black and slimy. The bark came off like dead skin. Branches caught at my jeans. The slash marks lay buried in the decomposing brush, and it was impossible to see the trail on the other side. We'd just have to hope it didn't veer off one way or another.

Sally heaved her pack over a five-foot trunk, hoisted herself up, and slid down the other side. "Is this fun for you?"

"Hell, no," I said.

"It is for me."

"Why?"

"Because I'm doing it with someone I really like." Midway over another slimy log, she gave me an earnest smile.

"Well, apart from that..." I said.

"There is no 'apart from that'. Who you're with makes all the difference."

When I was younger I might have thought that. Now, it felt like life and who you were with was more a matter of endurance. Marriage was a hole you fell into, but couldn't escape, no matter how hard your fingers clawed at the crumbling bank.

Almost to the other side of the avalanche, she spotted where the trail resumed: a slash mark on a standing pine. After the switchbacks and seven hundred feet of elevation gain that came next — a long, hard and exhausting slog — I knew we would be home free; but, I feared that with all the snow we had walked through and all the snow still on the peaks, the water in Evolution Creek was going to be too damn cold to cross safely.

The trail ended at the water's edge. I walked up and down the bank, looking for the ford. Evolution Creek fed the south fork of the San Joaquin, and its roar hurt my ears. Actually, "creek" was the wrong word. "River" was more accurate.

"Did you bring a rope?" I shouted.

Sally shrugged off her pack and pulled loops of climbing rope from the sleeping bag compartment. "A hundred foot."

I said, "I'll go across first and come back for our packs."

"If I've got a rope, " she said, "I think I can make it over without your help."

"The water's too deep. You'll be off balance. Listen to me for a change."

"Okay, fine. We'll do it your way."

Sally tied the rope to a tree.

I stripped down to the tighty-whities, stowed my clothes, and put my boots back on. With the water rushing so fast, all I'd need was to cut my foot on a rock.

She looked me up and down, the corner of her mouth curling.

I put a hand on my chest. "What?"

"You idiot." She shook her head. "Do you really want to go first?"

"You're not that good a swimmer."

"Try not to get hypothermia."

"Agreed."

As I stepped into the creek, the first shock of cold made

my nuts shrink up. I looked back. She stood sober-faced on the bank, playing out the coils of rope. The current felt like a gale-force wind. I would have been scared to go downriver on a raft; but walking and being careful where I planted my boots, I made it across and tied off the rope. The tension in the line made it easier for me to carry our packs. With the rope under my arm, I felt steadier. Even so, when I stumbled out after my third trip, my chest ached with the effort it took to breathe.

Across the river, Sally stripped down to her sports bra and underpants. She untied the rope, looped it like a lariat, and stepped into the stream.

I cupped my hands. "Tie it back! Tie it back!"

Maybe she couldn't hear. The slack rope dropped in the water, and the current carried it downstream. To keep the tension, I coiled fast. Halfway over, Sally stepped in a depression, and the water made a collar around her neck. I pulled up the slack and hauled her to shore.

Soaked, spent, shivering, she threw herself on the meadow grass. "My husband would have let me drown."

Furious at her recklessness, I turned her on her back and pinioned her arms. "Why in hell did you untie the rope? Didn't you hear me?"

"I was afraid someone might follow us."

"Who?"

"My husband."

"Jesus, girl!" I collapsed on her and cried. It was the first time I had cried since Marge showed me that first and un-wanted pink test strip, and I could feel Sally's arms around me, rubbing my back.

"It's okay, John. We made it."

"Yeah, but…"

"We're safe. Nobody can get to us here."

Even with my body half frozen, I was utterly relieved to

have made it across the river. Sally tried to smooth out the goose bumps with her fingers. After a while, I stopped shaking, but I could still feel her fingers going up and down my spine and into the small of my back. Down my legs even. It was as if she was seeing me for the first time, but with her hands.

I moved off her and hunkered on all fours. She lay there, arms flung and legs spread and laughing like a crazy person. I was just about to tell her to stop it, for God's sake, when I noticed a brown pencil-like line heading south from her navel. The same line Margie had. Sally's stomach was flat. No stretch marks on her hips. None visible on her breasts. Through her bra, her tits looked like acorn caps, bumpy and brown.

She turned her head. "Long enough rest?"

I pointed to the brown line. "When did you lose the baby?"

She swallowed. "It was more than one."

"What, twins?"

"No, more than one time."

"Fixing to try again?"

She reached out for my hand, smiled, and nodded.

"What makes you think this time'll be different?"

"It will. I just know it." She rubbed my fingers against her face.

Her skin felt warm.

Scrambling to her feet, she took jeans and a shirt from her pack. "Let's go on up to the lake."

I changed into dry clothes. My boots immediately soaked my socks. Cold stiffened my fingers, and I fumbled to untie the half hitch on the rope.

"Leave it for when we come back." Sally said.

I did and hoisted on my pack. My teeth chattered.

We had hiked eight miles with Evolution Creek on our left. Now, it was on our right. The forest had thinned and the land flattened. Beyond an inundated meadow lay Evolution Lake, four miles long and ringed by granite peaks.

I found a camp spot on a little peninsula. There was a fire ring and level ground for our sleeping bags. I built a fire, tore open a packet of beef stroganoff, put water on to boil, and warmed my hands. While Sally hung our food bag, I checked the sleeping bags to see if they would zip together. My toes burned with cold, and I wanted to borrow some of her body heat.

"Hey," she called, pointing to the lake. "Don't miss the *Alpenglo*." She was already on her way, striding toward a granite boulder out on the tip of the peninsula.

I put the bags down.

Knit hats over our ears, we sat like two birds on a wire and stared at the still water of Evolution Lake; its shimmering surface filled me with peace. Off some ways, in a half-ring, stood four big, snow-covered peaks — Mounts Huxley, Spencer, Darwin, and Mendel. To my knowledge, not one of those great men had talked about love, as if the survival of the human race depended only on the practical stuff — who would bring home the woolly mammoth and who would cook it — but, my life had shown me that all that "survival of the species" stuff is driven by our bodies' needs, who we yearn for and who we cannot do without.

"I'm going to check on the fire," I said.

"Don't be too long," she said.

"I won't."

The fire had dried my socks, and I pulled them over my hands. When I returned, I sat next to her, an arm around her shoulder.

"What's this?" She wiggled the sock's toe. "A wool condom?"

I laughed. "You're lucky to be alive. You know that?"

She cuddled against me. "I know." Then, after a pause, "Glad, too."

"You had something to tell me."

She didn't move, but I felt her stiffen. A fish jumped right in front of us. The ripples settled.

"There were five altogether," she said.

"Five babies?"

"Yes," she said.

"How far along were you?"

"Heard a heartbeat on the last one."

I exhaled and it came out like a whistle. She was thirty-nine.

"You sure you want to try again?" I said.

"I don't want to be having a baby just to have a baby," she said. "I want to be a mother, to raise a child and watch it grow. The problem is, my husband won't touch me."

"What a fool."

Although, to give her husband the benefit of the doubt, maybe he couldn't stand to see her suffer.

I took off my sock and laced my fingers through hers. She squeezed back. I wanted her for more than one night. I wanted her in a motel room where we could sleep with the covers off and wake up to coffee and hot showers. I wanted her for as long as it would take us to make a baby, and for more nights after that. And, if that happened, I wanted to keep her off horses, at least until she came to term, even though asking her to leave the mountains would be like asking her to peel off her skin.

I took her chin and turned her face toward mine. Her lips felt cold and dry. As the sun went down, all the blues, greens, and browns of the sky changed into the red glow of battered, cutthroat trout on their mating run upstream.

How confusing it was to be human. How surprising. This moment was one I had waited for my entire life.

HUNGER

———o———

S O DECADENTLY RICH, the taste and texture of hot
chocolate. The heavy white porcelain mug, the froth of
bubbles and fresh nutmeg, but most of all, the spoonable res-
idue at the bottom. Just beyond the mahogany doors of the
American Express Global Lounge was the best hot chocolate
in the whole wide world. Olympia Stavropoulis, pulling her bag
of pharmaceutical brochures, held her phone above the scanner
at the scanner at the check-in counter. A nervous craving, not
hunger exactly, but a feeling similar to hunger, overcame her
before international flights.

Inside the lounge, Olympia, gold hoop earrings jangling
against the collar of her flowing cape, brushed past the business
travelers relaxing on leather couches. She had expected more of
a reaction — a cocked head; eyes taking her measure — because
she was careful about how she presented herself and wanted to
come off as a woman of substance. The purple cape was a state-
ment not just of grandeur but of practicality, for it was often
true that in coach, the blankets did not quite cover her body,
and the soft wool kept her from freezing beneath the whistling
nozzles that blew cold air. But, never mind. A job was a job,
for her as much as for anyone else, and she could endure the

18

indignities of the flight: crowded bins, snoring seatmates, and most of all, tiny portions of food. She considered grabbing a few of the pastry-wrapped Vienna sausages put out as snacks, but decided against it. Just get the chocolate, she told herself, then on to the gate.

At the bar, she parked one buttock on a stool. The bar was manned by a trim blond, his face half-hidden by dangling wine glasses. High intensity lights shaped like upside-down waffle cones lit her diamond ring.

"I'd like some hot chocolate, please," she said.

"No can do," the bartender said. "The machine is broken."

"But you don't need a machine to make chocolate," Olympia said. "All you need is a pan and some hot milk."

"We make our *cocoa* with an espresso machine."

"You grind the beans from scratch?"

"From scratch."

"I walked all the way down here to get chocolate, and now you don't have it? You guys have the best chocolate in the world, right here in this bar, and now I know why. You grind the beans. Imagine that!"

"Sorry to disappoint," the bartender said, wiping lipstick from a glass. "Can I get you something else? A chardonnay, perhaps?"

"Let me think." Was there something else she craved? Not really. She had counted on chocolate to help her sleep. At bedtime her grandmother, a wiry-haired widow who spoke not a word of English, had always given her a warm cup of Nestle's Quik. The bedtime ritual had become a habit. A warm drink relaxed the body and calmed the mind.

"How about a decaf? Cream and sugar," she said.

"Coming right up." A moment later the bartender placed the mug of coffee on the counter and handed her packets of creamer.

"Could I have real cream?" she asked. "I don't want to scald my tongue."

"Sure," he said, turning to take a carton of half-and-half from a small refrigerator.

Pouring the cream, she hoped the residual amount of caffeine in the coffee wouldn't keep her awake. She was off to eastern Europe for another round of show-and-tell, peddling out of date drugs to government clinics. She hated the beaten down look of the beleaguered doctors, their haggard, hollow eyes. Cows, she thought. Sheep. Hunger for the drugs was the only detectable glow in their anxious eyes.

"I live in Chicago," she said, "and once a year I take a vacation for two weeks. I go on cruises. The last time I went up the Inland Passage. Do you know it? It was spectacular, all those glaciers crashing into the sea! And I go back to Greece every five or six years to see my parents' relatives, who are all dying off. They live on olive farms overlooking the sea, but the streets are all stone, and I usually twist my ankle and end up being carried around the town in a straight-backed chair. Like one of the Madonna statues they carry around on feast days." She laughed. "It's really pretty hilarious."

"You must rack up the frequent flier miles."

"Too many to count."

"What do you do?" he asked.

"I sell drugs to third world countries. I've had the Asian market until recently, but China's been making more and more cheap drugs — knockoffs, like they do with computer programs or CDs. They have little sweatshops where they crank out insulin and antibiotics and old standbys like Valium and Prozac. It seems the whole world is on anti-depressants. 'Course nobody knows the quality of the drugs. The Chinese say they're the same. They don't really test them or anything. A bunch of people got sick in Denmark last year. Turned out they'd mixed in some barrels of drugs from China with product from the Czech Republic, and it made a supremely toxic cocktail. Do you believe that?"

The bartender looked down in the sink. Olympia saw that the suds had gone flat and the water turned gray. So much for hygiene.

"When I was young my mother said I should guard my independence," she said.

"Meaning what?" the bartender said.

"Meaning earn my own money. Don't get pushed into marriage. Now she's singing a different tune. Why don't you ever date? Where are my grandchildren? My mother says it would be cheaper for me to rent a hotel. She's probably right. I've been doing this for three years. I can't keep a houseplant alive. Isn't that pathetic?"

The bartender pulled the plug. The sink emptied, and Olympia heard a slurp from the drain.

The bartender picked up a hand towel. "Lady, you've been on the road too long."

OLYMPIA HAD TO admit she was quite fagged out from traveling. The hotels of eastern Europe offered the desultory service of formerly state-run enterprises — smoke-saturated rooms and green cornflakes in the breakfast buffet. No air conditioning. Of course, the company could have put her up at a Hilton, but the Hiltons were near the tourist sites, and she wasn't there to be a tourist.

At the gate her name appeared on a list of passengers awaiting upgrades, but she had little hope of getting one. First-class seats filled early on overseas flights. Besides the ability to stretch out and lie flat, an amenity that might have allowed her to sleep on the plane, a first-class meal was better than the food in most restaurants in Budapest, where the meat, gristly and overcooked, swam in goulash.

"You're in luck, Miss Stavropoulis," the gate attendant said. "Your upgrade has been approved."

"It has?" she gasped. This was her lucky day. But then she'd earned it. As the bartender said, she'd been on the road too long. Once upon a time, back when she was in her twenties and struggling to finish an MBA, she had imagined a man in her life. Maybe children. These she had traded for acquaintances, money, and what could pass for respect. If she occasionally had doubts about whether selling drugs was a meaningful way to live a life, well, no point in second-guessing.

The flight began to board. Now she gave herself permission to be pampered, just as she had given herself permission to buy her own diamond ring. She settled comfortably into her window seat, and the flight attendant offered sparkling champagne. She suddenly no longer missed the foregone hot cocoa.

At the last minute before takeoff, a woman, likely in her late seventies, arms loaded with packages, made a great bustle getting on board. She insisted the flight attendant fit her packages in the overhead bin and hang her fur coat (a mink, if Olympia was any judge). The woman tottered on her spike heels, her thin ankles bowed. After sitting down briefly, the woman suddenly stood and began to rummage around in the luggage bin. Oh, great. A fussbudget, Olympia thought. The stewardess asked the woman to take her seat — the flight was about to take off — but the woman said there was a mirror in her carry-on, and she wanted to freshen her face. Unable to hide her annoyance, the flight attendant took down the carry-on and waited while the woman located the mirror. Once she found it, she sat down. It was ridiculous to worry about how you looked on a plane. In the airport, okay. But on an overnight flight? Why had the woman insisted on getting her mirror?

The woman's seat faced the front of the aircraft and Olympia's the rear. A glass panel divided the two seats. Olympia decided to leave the panel down. She was curious.

Loose strands of white-blond hair had escaped the net of the woman's chignon, and she dampened her fingers, setting them right. Like a robber wearing a nylon stocking, the woman's features were smooth but flattened. Makeup caked in the creases around her mouth. The woman outlined her lips with a lip brush, making the contour wider than the lips themselves. A perimeter of fine lines around her mouth suggested that she'd spent all seventy plus years smoking.

Glancing at Olympia, the woman grimaced and tucked her lip brush in her purse. "I hate to put on my face in public." She had a voice like twanging string, and Olympia was glad she did not go on. If she had, Olympia would have raised the divider, which would have sent a less than subtle message, but too bad. It was a long flight. She felt an aversion for the visible loneliness of nonstop talkers. Or was it narcissism? There was something not quite right about this woman, and Olympia began to speculate about her possible lives, always so much more interesting than the actual life the woman probably did lead. Besides hot chocolate, which Olympia had not managed to get, coming up with theories about the psychology of her fellow travelers was the one thing she enjoyed about her job. That, and the money, of course.

The seat belt sign came on.

The woman pulled her seat belt tight across the wrinkles in her skirt. The woman's hips were only half as wide as the seat. She looked like one of those rich, spindly old ladies you read about who start writing checks to strangers, a woman with many acquaintances, but no true friends. But who was Olympia to talk?

The woman leaned into the aisle and, waving a heavily veined and bejeweled hand, called forward. "Miss, bring me a whiskey sour."

Olympia watched cartoon people on her individual screen go through the safety drill: no smoking in the lavs; keep computers and cell phones off until ten thousand feet; put oxygen masks on children before putting on your own. Blah, blah, blah.

The woman rested her hand on the divider, addressing first Olympia and then the flight attendant, who had returned with a napkin and drink.

"I've had a frightful ordeal," the woman said across the divider. "I am just shaking from the stress of getting on this flight."

This will be a difficult customer, Olympia thought.

"Bad traffic getting to the airport?" The stewardess spoke placatingly, as she would to an unaccompanied minor. She herself was in her mid-twenties, a petite brunette in just enough make up.

"No traffic at all." The old woman turned to Olympia. "I bought my ticket at the last minute. Can you believe they charged me $8,225?"

Olympia choked on her champagne. "I hope that's round trip."

"No, it's one way."

"Why didn't you travel coach?"

The woman pursed her lips and frowned. "One can't really fly in coach, can one?"

"One could if one had to,'" Olympia muttered.

Olympia always flew coach because her trips often had to be arranged at the last minute. Surplus drugs had a tendency to pop up on the market unannounced, and she had to scurry over to Europe and try to sell them, or they would have gone to the landfill.

"EXCUSE ME," THE flight attendant said. "Would you like a hot towel?"

Olympia opened her eyes and took a washcloth from the

tongs. Damp heat seeped into her pores. The good thing about this flight was that she had no paperwork. All that could wait until Hungary. Meanwhile, whatever food was being warmed in the galley smelled awfully good.

"Would you prefer salmon or sirloin?" the flight attendant said, her pencil poised to take a note.

"Salmon, please," Olympia said.

"That's the last salmon," the stewardess said, her eyes bright. She turned to the other woman. "Will sirloin be fine?

"I don't eat beef," the woman said.

"Are you vegetarian?"

"No. I eat fish. I need the calcium."

The stewardess walked backwards a few paces and addressed the entire cabin. "We have a pescatarian onboard. Would anyone be willing to change the salmon entrée for beef?"

Olympia heard mumbles that sounded like "What the hell's a pescatarian?" but otherwise no response.

The stewardess returned with a wicker basket to collect the towels.

"I paid over $8,000 for my ticket," the woman said. "You should have all selections available."

"Let me just check again." The flight attendant went back to the galley.

Olympia heard her clanking about and discussing the matter with the other attendants.

Olympia wasn't about to give up her salmon voluntarily. This was a treat she deserved. She wasn't fond of beef, even in the best of times, and it was never cooked right on an airplane. Too well done and stringy.

"I just recounted the dinners." The flight attendant's voice came over the loudspeaker. She had picked up the galley phone. "It seems we're one dinner short. Please ring your call button if you'd be willing to volunteer for a coach dinner."

Papers rattled. Throats cleared. No one volunteered.

A moment later the stewardess stood by their seats. She looked from Olympia to the woman. "Since you were last on board, I wonder if you would help us out by taking a coach meal."

"I paid $8,000 for my ticket!" Visibly flustered, the woman snapped, "I insist on a first-class meal."

"Please," the stewardess cajoled. "We're happy to give you all the alcohol you want."

"I don't want to get drunk. I want the meal I paid for."

The woman's complaint could be heard throughout the cabin. Olympia turned and saw heads nodding in solidarity. The plane had leveled off, but the seat belt sign remained on. The woman unbuckled. "I want to talk to the Captain."

"The Captain's flying the plane," the stewardess said, stiffening and spreading her arms to the adjoining seats.

The woman stood and, shakily, ducked beneath the flight attendant's arm. In the galley a male flight attendant attempted to intercept her, but she slipped past and banged on the cockpit's door.

"Open up," she demanded. "I need to speak to the Captain."

The steward attempted to guide her back to her seat, but she pounded his chest and clawed his face. The stewardess picked up the phone to talk to the Captain. Olympia heard snatches of conversation.

Did this woman think a dinner would fly through the air and suddenly fill the vacant spot in the warming oven?

The male steward, holding a towel to his scratch, told the woman, "Take your seat immediately, or we'll have the police waiting for you when we land."

"I paid for a first class dinner." The woman hunched over, chin dimpled, mouth trembling. "It's not fair."

"Life's not fair. Come along now," the steward said, adding under his breath, "you old bitch."

She went meekly, obedient only to a man it seemed, and once back in her seat, sat like a child put in detention, her expression wounded and defiant. She finished her drink and ordered another.

Returning with a glass of merlot, the flight attendant eyed both Olympia and her seatmate with a frown, her look of disapproval lingering on Olympia. No way was Olympia going to admit that her upgrade had caused the cabin to come up one meal short.

At last the stewardess brought dinner. The old woman stared at her coach meal — peas and carrots, mashed potatoes, and a small portion of overcooked beef. She sighed and squeezed her temples. Then she began to cry, those big, gulping sobs Olympia remembered from her school days: the playground's class warfare. Olympia had never bullied girls in lower grades, but she recognized that such people existed: thin-skinned, fragile girls with no defenses. Such girls grew up and never learned to fend for themselves.

"Oh, come on. It's not as bad as all that." Olympia reached over the divider and exchanged the woman's meal for her own. "Dry your eyes."

The woman looked at the salmon. "That's very kind." She picked up a cocktail napkin and blotted her cheeks. "Your good deed shall not go unrewarded. I'll write you a check after dinner."

"Don't be silly," Olympia said.

"Are you sure?"

"Very."

Finally, the woman conceded and unwrapped her silverware.

Olympia watched, dismayed, as the woman picked at the salmon and ratatouille and couscous so artfully arranged on the china plate. How was it possible, she wondered, for a person to hunger for a dish she had no appetite to eat?

MONGOOSE

——o——

A S PER USUAL, her indomitable father delivered the summons through his wife. The call came from Amelia, and though Gwen Castleman had no particular desire to rush to his bedside, the news that prostate cancer had spread to hot spots in his brain, shoulders, and hips had stirred the demons of longing and regret. "You should come before it's too late," Amelia had said. Gwen, cell phone in one hand, was just finishing a plowing run. "Yes, all right." She nearly had to shout over the engine's rough idle. Vermont was still locked down with snow, but planes could get in and out. With a ticket promised at the Burlington airport, Gwen put aside her misgivings. Like it or not, convenient or not, this was something she had to do.

After arriving in San Francisco, she took an Uber to Hillsborough and lowered her window for a better view of the live oaks, Mexican palms, and Japanese maples. Plants thrived. Gwen was a plant person, more at home outdoors than in. What had compelled her to move three thousand miles away and so rarely return?

At the foot of her father's driveway, she shouldered her backpack and trudged uphill. The stucco ranch house had a wide front porch, commanding view of the bay, and a solid mahogany door. Knocking, she felt a bit of a fraud, the dutiful daughter rushing to her dying father's bedside when her conscience told her it was not her father's death that had brought her all this way, but an animal desire to shed her heavy coat, the problems at home, and, however briefly, soak up some sun. Now that she was here, however, she felt like a loose balloon, floating up, disconnected from her life. She should be home plowing parking lots, not foisting the work off on her friends.

Inside, slippers shushed. The door opened, revealing a braless, heavyset Asian woman, her hair shoe-polish black and chopped off at the ears. The orange hibiscus on her muumuu did little to brighten the pallor of her skin.

"Is Mrs. Castleman here?" Gwen said.

"Marshall must be right," the woman laughed. "I'm letting myself go."

"Amelia?"

"Yes, it's me. The very same." Amelia made the sign of the cross and kissed her thumbnail.

Shades of tan and brown had mottled Amelia's fleshy arms, and fatigue had bruised her eyes. "Holy cow!" Gwen said. "I didn't recognize you."

Amelia attempted a wan smile. "Thanks be to God he hasn't completely worn me out."

"No, my bad," Gwen said.

"It's all right. Would you mind removing your shoes?"

"Of course."

Glad for a reason to bend over and hide her burning face, Gwen unlaced her boots. How fast things changed.

FIVE YEARS AGO, stopping on the way to a trade show in Montreal, her father Marshall had introduced Amelia, his fourth wife, all of them having been beauties. Gwen's mother, now deceased, had come first.

Marshall's visit had been a fly by. Meet for dinner in Burlington. No request to stay at her house or even see it. Gwen showed him pictures of the life she'd constructed: her Ford F-150, outfitted with a plow; the cabin she'd recently re-chinked; her garden with its towering sunflowers; the rescue shelter where she volunteered; and the phone bank where she'd raised money for Bernie's campaign.

She'd expected some reaction. Isn't there a man in your life? How do you support yourself? Instead, in a tit for tat, he had elbowed Amelia. "Show her the Oahu pictures."

"Honestly, Dad, it's wrong to order her around," Gwen said.

"I don't take it personally," Amelia said, but her weak shrug told Gwen that she did mind, even though she didn't dare admit it.

Born the same month and year, though under different signs, Gwen and Amelia had nothing in common except her father. Amelia was a Filipina who had grown up on one of Oahu's pineapple plantations. She had daughters living on the island. She had been Marshall's third wife's hairdresser, but when Wanda died, Marshall started coming in for a trim. "And the rest is history," Amelia said with a warm smile, reaching for his hand.

Back then, Amelia had looked like one of the girl-brides old men meet in chat rooms: a thin woman in Shantung silk, her red fingernails decorated with glitter. In a room of flannel-shirted diners, Amelia drew stares.

Soon after the wedding, Christmas presents began to appear, the first since she'd moved back East. Finding the gifts offensive, Gwen returned the unopened bread machine and assemble-it-yourself teak garden bench. Assuming Amelia had selected them, she sent a note saying she bought her bread from an artisan bakery and that she was morally opposed to cutting down tropical forests to make garden furniture, thank you very much. She knew that sounded bitchy, but honestly, the gifts were a direct assault on her core values. Protect the environment. Live a simple life. Accept nothing from her father.

She had thought that would be the end of it, but a week later Marshall called. "Your card hurt Amelia's feelings."

"Why is it I always have to worry about the delicate feelings of your wives?" Gwen asked.

She had not heard from him since. Not a card. Not a call. No more Amazon boxes showing up on her cabin porch, the cabin a chimney fire had so recently reduced to rubble. Since then she'd been couch-surfing at friends' houses, battling the insurance adjuster, and waking up at 3 a.m. to complete her plowing run. Scared and overwhelmed, (the Uber ride from the airport had cost more than a week's groceries) she wondered how — or even if — she could wrangle her life back to normal.

STANDING IN HER sweater, jeans, and wool socks, Gwen looked around the living room. An Oriental screen hung above an Italian leather couch. Her father had outlived each of his wives, but their decorating touches remained.

"I ought to rope this room off," Amelia said.

"It's a veritable shrine to the Wanda years," Gwen said.

Neither could hold back a knowing chuckle.

"Are you anxious to see your dad?" Amelia said.

"More like anxious in general."

"Why?"

"It's just a little strange to be here."

"I'll show you to your room. You can settle in and relax."

"It's hardly *mine*."

"Your dad always calls it 'Gwen's room,' so I guess I thought that had some significance."

"Maybe to him."

Gwen's mother had died midway through her senior year,

so her father had been forced to take her in. Right after graduation, she had accepted a summer job with the Forest Service and never returned.

Gwen dropped her backpack on the bed. Same spread. Brown twill. Not a very "girlie" room. Prior to her arrival, this room had been his home office. Castleman Industries, manufacturer of extrusions for vinyl replacement windows. The gunmetal-gray desk and filing cabinets were still there, along with the twin bed where she'd slept, facing a floor-to-ceiling mural of a forest. Yellow and amber leaves had fallen to the forest floor, and ferns grew among the trees.

Sarah, whom Gwen still thought of as her official stepmother, had said, "You're only living here till you go to college. Don't tape up any posters." After Sarah came Wanda, and now Amelia. It had taken Gwen a long time to sort out the puzzle pieces of blame and recrimination that, she supposed, happened after any divorce.

"How is Dad anyway? Did the doctors give you a timeline?"

Amelia frowned. "That's a strange way to put it."

"I'm sorry. The news came at me out of the blue. I haven't had time to process it."

"The hospice people say two to three months."

"I wish I'd known he wasn't at death's doorstep."

"You'd rather I'd waited for the funeral?"

"Not exactly, but winter is my busy season. The money I make now has to last the rest of the year."

She supposed he would leave her some money in his will, and she would look like an ingrate if she didn't put in an appearance. Not that anyone else would know, but she would know, and whatever she did or did not feel for him, he was still her father.

HE LAY MOTIONLES, his skin mottled and crosshatched

by wrinkles. Gwen knelt on the floor and rested her forearms on the mattress. The hot chocolate of his once-brown eyes had skimmed over, and the outline of his gums showed through his cheeks. With his every breath, she smelled the damp, fecund rot of compost. She covered her nose.

Amelia climbed onto the mattress and crawled over until she hovered above him. "You've got company!" she sang out.

"Hi, Dad," Gwen said, girding herself for his appraisal.

His eyes made a circuit of the room. To the right stood his-and-hers closets behind their bi-fold doors. Next came a bureau piled with linen. Then the hospital bed and bathroom door.

His eyes returned to Amelia's face. "What is the habitat of the mongoose?"

Frowning, Gwen settled back on her heels. "What's that supposed to mean?"

"I was dreaming about a mongoose," he said, never taking his eyes off Amelia.

"Maybe he's thinking about Ewa Plantation," Amelia said.

"What's Ewa Plantation?" Gwen said.

"Where I grew up." Amelia reached back and tweaked Marshall's toes. "Goosey, goosey, gander."

"I'm serious," he said.

"All right, Marshall. I hear you."

"Da-ad!" Gwen said, perplexed and frustrated.

His eyes flew back and forth, as if following the flight of a gnat.

Amelia plumped the pillows, and then backed off the bed. "He doesn't recognize you."

"Is that what's going on?" Gwen asked, somewhat offended and not wanting to let herself be hurt.

Whispering, Amelia crooked her finger. "Let him rest. You and I need to talk."

When they were in the kitchen with its round maple table and captain's chairs, Gwen let herself take a deep breath. Her legs shook and she sat, ducking to avoid the Tiffany chandelier. "I can't believe I came out here for this."

Amelia poured glasses of pineapple juice and brought them over. "The doctor says he has sundown syndrome. He gets his nights and days mixed up."

"Thanks." Gwen took a sip of the sweet juice. "Is he always so out of it?"

"If I cut back his morphine, he'll stop speaking nonsense, but then he's in a lot of pain."

"What's with the mongoose?"

"God only knows." Amelia shook her head, her eyes downcast.

An ancient, complete set of the *Encyclopedia Britannica,* bought years before from a door-to-door salesman, sat in its two-tiered, angled rack. Gwen pried the MA-MO free, the back creaking as she cracked it open. Marshall had bought the set for her, he claimed, but had kept it for himself.

"Are you looking up 'mongoose'?" Amelia carried her juice around and leaned with the other hand on Gwen's chair.

"It's just such a strange thing to mention. And, why 'habitat'?" Gwen turned the book sideways. A ferret-sized animal stood over a nest, its mouth dripping raw egg.

Amelia ran her index finger down the page. "'The mongoose was introduced into Hawaii to control snakes. The predators depleted native birds.' True, but not the whole story." Amelia straightened up and massaged her back. "Our mongoose died of snake bite."

"I thought they *ate* snakes."

"Just the eggs." Amelia checked her watch. "I have to give your dad his meds, and then I need to get some sleep. If I could just get him to move to the hospital bed, it would help so much.

I haven't slept more than an hour at a time for months. Oh, but listen to me. Complaining, complaining. I'm sorry. I'm not being very hospitable, but that's the reality."

"I'm tired, too." Gwen said. It had been a very long flight, and it was going on nine o'clock, midnight her time.

"Feel free to microwave a Lean Cuisine," Amelia said.

"No, thanks," Gwen said. "They fed me on the plane."

GWEN WOKE TO a view of the woods: the mural at the foot of her bed. Every fall, the forest in Vermont burst into a tapestry of color. Funny. She'd thought her move back East had been a fluke, a transfer from one region of the Forest Service to another; but no. Long before she understood that Vermont existed and that she could live there, this mural had given her the vision of a place to heal.

Speaking of which, what was going on back there? She picked up her phone from the floor. A message had come in. "Storm expected. Weather Service says BIG ONE. I'll do my best by your clients, but get back ASAP."

Good grief. Just what she didn't need. Her friend Ryan worked for a towing company which was why she'd asked him to cover. If her truck got stuck in snow, he'd be able to get it out. A storm, however, might very well mean he'd be out on the highway helping stranded skiers, and he wasn't such a good friend that she could expect him to completely pick up the slack. Maybe she should just fly home. Keep her customers happy. Keep fighting through the nightmare of insurance and the temptation to call her life a total loss. Besides, Amelia had everything under control.

She heard a thud from across the hall.

"All *right*, Marshall," Amelia said, the edge in her voice muffled by the bedroom doors. "Hold your horses."

Sounded like Amelia could use a hand after all.

Gwen pulled on yesterday's jeans, grabbed a tee shirt, and opened the door.

Amelia, dressed in a navy pantsuit, hugged an armload of dirty sheets. "He soaked the bed."

"Does he do that often?"

"Three times a day. Since you're here, would you stay with him while I go to Mass?"

"I thought Mass was on Sunday."

"It's Saturday, too."

"What do I have to do?"

"Just keep him company."

"What if he needs something?"

"He shouldn't. I changed him, and he's had a bit of oatmeal and juice. And, besides, you two need to get reacquainted."

With that Amelia headed off down the hall. A moment later the slam of the washer lid told Gwen that Amelia had started the laundry.

Gwen ran her hands down her braid. Her father hated that braid, said it made her look like a coolie. Quickly she undid the rubber band and finger-combed her hair. Then she knocked. "May I come in?"

"Who's that?"

She pushed the door. It swung in. "Your daughter."

His eyes ran up and down her body. She saw him watch her every step. She came around the foot of the bed and stood beside him. If he had ordered her to disrobe, she could not have felt more exposed.

"How the pigeons come home to roost!" he said.

That old awkwardness. Her hands swung like buckets. "You wanted to see me?"

"I *what?*"

"Wanted to see me."

Glasses slipped down the bridge of his nose. "Hell, you look

36

old."

Old prune! Let him stew in his own damn juice.

"I don't appreciate being insulted," she said. "Vermont's cold, and my job takes me out in all kinds of weather." She turned to leave.

"Don't run away." He clawed for her arm.

She pulled it away. "Did you want to see me or not?"

"No," he said. "But now that you're here, make yourself useful."

"How?" she said, hiding her resentment at being ordered around by this confused, and confusing, man, a shadow of his former strong and assured self.

"Go get the paper."

"Where will I find it?"

"On the porch if that good-for-nothing newspaper kid hasn't thrown it in the bushes. Where'd Amelia run off to?"

"Mass," Gwen said.

"When will she be back?"

"After Mass, I assume."

"All right. Go get the paper. Then I have something you can help me do."

She found the paper in the ivy and brought it to him.

He flapped the pages and held them in front of his face. A straight-backed chair sat next to the bathroom door. She pulled it over. Long ago, in sessions with a primal scream therapist, she had poured out her feelings to an empty chair.

"Dad, if you have anything to say to me, you'd better say it now. I'm leaving tomorrow."

He let out an exaggerated sigh and put down the paper. "What am I supposed to say?"

"I don't know."

"I guess you expect some kind of apology for me ruining your life."

"You didn't ruin my life."

"Then why are you so angry all the time?"

"I'm not angry. To be angry, I'd have to give a shit."

He tossed the paper aside. "I need a shave." He rubbed his chin and threw back the sheet.

His hospital gown had hiked up. She wasn't prepared for the sight: a garter belt circled his waist. Attached to it was a triangle of blue that reminded her of the absorbent pads that had protected her mother's bed. Veins twined up the shrunken muscles of his thighs, a sight that left her woozy and lightheaded.

"Should you be getting up?" she said.

"Just give me a hand." He slid his feet toward the edge of the bed.

Trying not to touch his horned toenails, she slid on his slippers, and then guided his arm around her shoulder, helping him to his feet. "Lean on me." He was emaciated, but dense, and supporting him from the side threw her off balance.

Panting in her ear, he bellowed, "Goddamn it!" His free hand seized the rail of the hospital bed.

She tried to walk him past it. When she pulled, he resisted.

"Wait," he said. "I need to rest."

"I thought you wanted to shave."

"Rest. First."

"All right." She pried his fingers off the guardrail, lowered it, and sat him backwards on the bed. Scooping up his legs, she swiveled him around.

The furnace fan kicked in, the vent right above his head.

"You're right in a draft," she said.

"Pull the sheet over me."

She removed his slippers. "Are you okay? Do you want to sit up?"

He shook his head, closing his eyes.

"How about if I shave you here?" she said.

"You can try." Though his hair had whitened, it still grew thick and full.

She found an electric razor in the medicine cabinet and wrapped a towel around his neck. Tilting his chin back, she separated the folds of skin. It was like mowing a field of dandelion fluff.

She turned off the razor and wiped his chin.

He opened his eyes. "Bring me my wallet."

"Why? You going shopping?"

"Thanks, and no. Apparently, I pick lousy gifts. The 'return to sender' kind."

Had he really picked out the bread machine and teak bench? She couldn't believe it. If she'd known that, she might have kept them, or at the very least, not sent such a nasty note. "Where would I find your wallet?"

"In the top drawer of the bureau. And get me some pillows."

"Don't you ever say 'please'?"

"Occasionally."

She put a pillow behind his head, then fished the electronic control from beneath the bed.

He played with the control and turned the bed into a recliner. "Say, this is swell! Much better than our bed." Sitting upright, he emptied the wallet in his lap. Credit cards scattered.

She picked them up.

"I wanted to show you something," he said, "but I must have lost it."

"What are you looking for?"

"A picture," he said.

She took the wallet and removed the cash. There, lodged in the corner of an inside flap, she found a kindergarten photo of herself, a stocky little girl with black bangs and a scowl. Kindergarten was when her parents' marriage had begun to collapse.

She held the picture for him to see. "Is this it?"

"Good girl." He took it and cupped it in his hand. "My little princess," he said tenderly.

Princess! Good grief. She tucked the credit cards back in their sleeves. Once, as a little girl, she had snuggled against him, an open book in her lap, listening to him read tales of princesses and knights in shining armor. After she'd outgrown being a princess, he hadn't known quite what to do with her.

His eyes closed. The picture fell from his hand. She raised the guardrail and slipped the picture in her pocket. Her life had been no fairy tale, but then neither had his.

WHEN SHE CAME into the kitchen looking for coffee, Gwen saw that Amelia had come straight back from church, thrown the sheets in the dryer, and put bowls of granola on the table.

"Sit! Sit!" Amelia broke off a banana and took a knife from the drawer.

"I don't see how you do this," Gwen said, settling into a captain's chair.

"I just tell myself he's a mongoose."

"In what way?" Gwen asked, pouring milk on her cereal.

"Fearless."

"But how is that like a mongoose?"

Amelia brought coffee and sliced bananas to the table and sat. "I wanted to tell you the story last night, but I got distracted."

"What story?"

"The story of our mongoose."

Gwen scattered discs of bananas on her granola. "I'm listening."

"A poisonous snake moved to our village," Amelia said. "In quick succession, two children died from bites, and parents became scared to let their kids go into the fields. The children all had to stay in the confines of the village—thirty or forty kids — playing under the porches and in between the shacks of the common area. The grownups grew tired of the racket. They wanted us kids to roam freely, the way we had done before. Instead of keeping his eye on the workers, my father, who was the overseer, took the mongoose out every day. They hunted for the snake and its nest. Miraculously, the mongoose found the nest, but the snake, sleeping nearby, woke up suddenly, striking for my father's leg."

"Your father must have been terrified!"

"Oh, believe me, he froze. But the mongoose persisted, hissing and trying to attack. The snake turned its attention from my father to the mongoose. It struck again and again, each time spending more venom.

"My father got around behind the snake and chopped off its head with a hoe. He thought the mongoose would be all right on account of its thick coat, but with the snake dead, my father saw the venom start to act. The mongoose's legs stiffened, and it gasped for breath. The coat was thick, but the snake had bitten right through.

"My father carried the mongoose back to the village, sobbing as if he'd lost a child. From then on, anyone who acted bravely in the face of certain death, we called him a mongoose."

"Is your father still alive?"

"No. He passed."

"Did you take care of him?"

"Oh, yes. It is our obligation."

"For how long?"

"Seven years."

"And now you're doing it again."

"It won't go on forever."

"And then?"

"I will return to Oahu, cut hair, and spoil my grandkids."

"Don't you want to stay in my dad's house?"

"My people believe the ghosts of the newly departed linger."

Gwen spooned a second helping of bananas on her cereal. "Amelia, truly, you are an exceptional woman."

"Oh, not me. Your father is the mongoose of the house. He's lonely and scared, but never lets on."

Gwen reached into her pocket for the picture. "This is me at six."

Amelia examined the picture. Then she drew an imaginary circle around the eyes. "There's a lot of him in you."

"Let me see."

Gwen looked at the picture again. Her own young self — bristly, fearless, determined — stared back.

"Yes," she said. "I can see that."

INK

———○———

SPIKED GRAY MOUNTAINS surrounded the Valley of the Sun, and at its eastern fringe, subdivisions and trailer parks gave way to the Sonoran Desert. Ahead, over the Alero's sun-cracked dash, loomed the Superstitions' brooding, mahogany cliffs. It was Saturday. Just off the Higley exit, Layton Young, who had come to buy a car, turned his Alero into the Circle K. Beneath the mesquites planted in the berm, he spotted a white Hyundai Sonata. He parked and got out.

A heavyset man opened the Sonata's back door and swung one foot at a time onto the softening asphalt. Layton stopped in his tracks. Tattoos covered the man's head and the folds of his neck, and inky snakes covered the hand extended in greeting.

Layton stared at the hand, then shook it. "Hope I didn't hold you up," Layton said. "My manager kept us late."

"That's okay," the man said. "Anyway, thanks for making the trek out to Gilbert."

"I didn't think it would be this far."

"Higley's not that far."

"My buddy could have driven me to your house."

"Half the streets don't even show up on a GPS. Circle K's pretty convenient, huh? Right off the 60, just like I said, and it don't make no difference, you being late, 'cause I needed to put some gas in the tank. Now, she's all topped off and ready to go."

"I want to take a look first. Take it for a spin."

"Sure, sure." The tattooed seller nodded and stepped back.

Layton walked around the car. A shopping cart had dinged the door. The bumpers had a few scratches, but the tires still showed a good amount of tread.

"I ran the VIN number by CARFax," Layton said, "and it doesn't look like you had any accidents."

"I would have told you if we had," the seller said. "I hope you checked Bluebook. They say a 2010's worth $6300, but I'll take $4200, long as it's cash."

Layton reached for the inside pocket of his sport coat. "Can you take a check?"

"A cashier's check. Yeah, I'll take that."

"I didn't bring a cashier's check. All's I've got is a personal check."

"You gotta be kidding."

Layton looked toward the freeway. The roar of traffic spilled into the parking lot. "I guess I could give you cash, but my bank's in Tempe."

"I can follow you," the man said.

"It's 11:15."

"Let's make it snappy then. If you want it, that is."

Layton looked at the man again. The tattoos came over his head and ended just above his eyebrows.

"I have to admit that when you got out of the car, I kind of caught my breath," Layton said.

"Guess you're not into tattoos."

"Not really."

"They're not just for gangbangers and criminals."

Grimacing, Layton loosened his tie. "I wouldn't know."

"When people see me for the first time, they go, Whoa! But, actually, I'm not like that at all. I'm a pussycat. Just ask my wife."

The car had been idling all this time. The side windows of the sedan were tinted. Layton bent down to look in the driver's window. The front seats were empty.

"You have a wife?"

"Sure, I have a wife. What do you think?"

"Is this her car?"

"It was. Now it's gonna be yours."

"If you want to get to the bank—"

"Don't worry. We got time. Wait'll the wife comes back."

"Where is she?"

The man pointed to the Circle K. "Inside getting a Coke."

The convenience store's cantilevered overhang shaded its windows. They were dark and coated with dust. Plastic garbage cans stood on either side of the door. Customers moved from the gas pumps to the store and came out with bottled water and salty snacks.

"I wouldn't buy a car without a test drive," Layton said.

"Sure. Me neither. But unfortunately, I can't squeeze my ass behind the wheel. I mean, look at the vehicle. Koreans are small, right? You ever see a Korean my size?"

The man's belly formed a shelf beneath the slipcover of his shirt. He wore baggy jeans with ripped knees; his tennis shoes were unlaced, and he wore no socks. His round cheeks and relentless cheer turned his eyes to slits.

Layton pulled off his tie and wiped his brow with a handkerchief. "You into sumo wrestling?"

"Not particularly. Why'd you ask that?"

"I thought you might be into martial arts is all."

"Why, because of the shaved head?"

"Actually, your eyes are slanted."

The man frowned. "My eyes are not slanted. Where you getting that?"

"You kind of remind me of Leonard Peters."

"Should I know him?"

"He played safety for the Jets. My buddy and me met him in Hawaii. Can you believe he was performing Polynesian dances with flaming swords? He had a big old tattoo all across his chest and arm. Only you've got more of them."

A white Ram Charger squealed into the parking lot. The seller turned to look at it.

A highway worker wearing a hard hat and orange safety bib hopped down. He walked around to the truck bed, rooted around among the caution signs and tarps, and found two three-gallon thermoses. He carried them inside.

"What the fuck is my wife doing in there?" the tattooed man said.

"Maybe she fell in," Layton said.

"There's always a line for the women's."

"I swear you've got some Polynesian blood in you. Tongan, maybe. So, what are you anyhow?"

"I'm Mexican and German, if it makes any difference."

"Okay, I got it."

"You have to place people in categories? Everybody's got their little slot? Ker-ching, ker-ching?"

"I just want to know who I'm buying from."

"You're buying my wife's car. You're not even buying from me. I'm just the pimp."

"If you say so."

The sun had nearly reached its zenith, turning the air thick and close. The inked designs on the man's head looked like large commas. Some were red. Others blue. There were dots and crosshatches in contrasting colors.

"What are you staring at?" the man said.

"Your head kind of reminds me of one of my mom's old scarves."

"Now you're making fun of me."

"No, I'm not. I'm just curious about the design. Does that have some significance?"

The man ran a palm over his head. "It's hard to engrave a head with as much hair as mine has, so it was pretty much paisley or nothing. Once I broke free of the hair line, it was back to smooth skin." He lifted his shirt. "This here on my belly's Neptune with his triton, and below him — you can just see their heads poking up above my belt line — those are the Naiads."

"Like that woman who tried to swim from Cuba?"

The man dropped his shirt. "I don't know anything about any woman who tried to swim from goddamned Cuba. Mine come from Greek myths."

"Where'd you learn all this?"

"I was trained. I have a degree in graphic arts from ASU."

"My taxpayer dollars are training tattoo artists?"

"I wish you'd shut the fuck up. You're making me agitated. Christ, it must be a hundred and fifteen." The man turned his back and walked toward the berm where the trees provided some shade. He removed a red bandanna from his back pocket and mopped his brow and the back of his neck. "Say, what time's your bank close? Noon? We better book it, man."

Layton looked at his watch. "Actually, I think they might be open till two. Let me check my iPhone."

"What are you, some kind of computer geek?"

"I work in the GoDaddy call center."

"Man, I'd slit my fucking wrists."

"It wasn't what I ever planned to do."

"What did you plan to do?"

"I can't remember."

"You got amnesia, or you just don't want to tell me?"

Layton looked back at the car. Water puddled beneath it.

"You're wasting gas, letting it idle like that, and it's bound to overheat," Layton said. "If you're cooled off, maybe you could show me the car."

"All right. Let's start with the routine maintenance." The man opened the passenger door and took receipts from the glove box. Then he walked around to the driver's side, opened the door, and pointed to a sticker. "See, right there on the door's the oil change. Three thousand miles, like the dealer says. 'Course, I didn't take it to the dealer 'cause he'd just rip me off, right? My buddy, he does the maintenance in trade. He was all hot for this dragon I got winding up my arm." The man pushed one sleeve up to his shoulder. "Flex one way, and the head stretches out. My guy's got a forked red tongue, good for going down on a woman, you know?"

"I wouldn't have any idea."

"Oh, I'm sorry. That made you blush. Well, maybe you go down on men."

"I'm the Church of Jesus Christ— LDS— and we don't condone homosexuality."

The tattooed man smiled. "I've known Mormons who go down on men. They just don't advertise it."

Layton gave him a push. "Hey!"

"Oh, c'mon. Back off. I'm just having a little fun. Here, here, I gotta show you the wheel cover." He leaned inside and pointed. "I'm gonna throw it in for free. That's the little dragon there at ten o'clock. Over at two o'clock, you got Pisces and at four, Leo. If you're into astrology—"

"I'm not."

"No? What's your birthday?"

"None of your business."

The man held up both hands. "Whoa, whoa! I was just gonna tell you your sign."

"Show me the car."

"Let me pop the hood." The tattooed man turned off the engine, pocketed the key, and closed the driver's door. The hood latch clicked. He swung the prop into place. "Engine's clean. I topped off the washer fluid, so you're good to go."

Layton leaned over. The wiper fluid was full. The oil on the dipstick looked clean.

"What's that brown stuff all over the engine?"

"Oh, that's just dried mud. I took her out to an arroyo on the Beeline Highway. When there's a full moon, my wife and I have a cookout and then we fuck." He closed the hood. "Hear that slam? Car's tight. You can take her down to Tortilla Flat, and she'll float across the Verde River. Practically a pontoon boat."

"What are you going to do without a car?"

"See the tan Bronco?" The tattooed man pointed to an SUV in the opposite corner of the lot. "That's ours. It's a gas hog, but our kids like it better."

"You have kids?"

"The dogs, I mean."

"I always wanted dogs."

"Why don't you get one? My wife's going to breed ours. If all goes according to plan, she can sell you a puppy three months from now."

"What are they?"

"Mastiffs."

"Those are big dogs."

"Yeah, they eat a lot, and she just lost her job."

"Why'd she lose her job?"

"Two hundred people got laid off in her division."

"Oh, she got riffed."

"Yeah. It sort of sucks."

"What did she do?"

"She was processing files for that program Obama got going, the one where they have the kids submit proof they've been here since the day their parents walked across the desert. She was a file checker. They paid $18.50 an hour. Trump didn't like it. He cut it way back. Now, the only jobs in the newspaper say they'll pay $11 and no bennies, so we're pretty much back to square one. I told her it's either the house or the car, and she decided the dogs needed a yard."

The door of the Circle K opened. The construction worker came out. His head and shoulders were wet where he'd likely doused them in the men's room. He lowered the thermoses to the blistering asphalt. Squinting up at the sun, he lit a cigarette.

Layton shielded his eyes. "We've been standing out in the blazing sun for half an hour."

"All right, then. Get in the car and let's take 'er for a spin."

"You're going to trust me to drive?"

"Hell, yeah, man. I can fit in the back seat, just not the front. The way we work it is my wife drives, and I slide the passenger seat all the way forward. I wanted her to give you a tour of the dash, but you can read the manual."

"It's weird that you let her drive you around."

"It is not. It's just the way we do it." He handed Layton the key.

Layton got in the car. He adjusted the seat and mirrors.

The man opened the back door. His weight rocked the car. "All right. I'm in."

"Are you buckled up?"

"Actually, the seat belt's on the short side. Just go ahead and drive."

Layton turned the key. The dashboard showed the tank was full, the engine charging.

"I don't want to get a ticket," Layton said.

"The police don't care."

"I'll stay on Baseline."

"You can take her onto the highway."

"No, Baseline's okay." He backed up, and then eased out onto the road.

A moving van came up on his tail. He put on the flashers. The van changed lanes.

From the back seat, the man said, "What's important to you?"

Layton looked in the mirror. The man's smile had dropped away.

"What kind of question is that? You mean about what I wanted to be when I grew up?"

The man laughed. "I meant about the car."

"Oh, the car." Layton tested the horn and turn signal.

A stoplight turned red. The brakes grabbed.

"Well, I guess I should listen to the engine."

"You won't hear anything. It runs quiet."

"Yes. I can hear that. It's sort of a hum."

"You ever try yoga?"

"No."

"My wife likes yoga."

The signal changed.

"I'm going to head back."

"Don't worry. She'll wait for us."

Layton turned north and adjusted the vent louvers. Cool air blasted.

"So how do you make a living?" Layton said. "Do you have your own tattoo parlor or work for somebody?"

"It's my own parlor. I got binders full of designs. Dragons. Hot cars. Devils. Roses. Snakes. Hearts. Tigers. Tigers are big. Everybody wants a tiger, especially the Chinese. I have clients who fly in from Manhattan. The ones on my body, I didn't actually do myself. I did the design, but my assistants put them on."

Layton looked in the rearview mirror. The man took up half the back seat.

"Assistants? You mean you pay people? FICA and all that?"

"Depending on the business, yeah. Business is a little slow now, but it starts picking up in October. I'll be busy till the end of May."

"I wouldn't have thought that."

"Students'll be back. Then Canadians. Then spring training."

"It's cyclical, then."

"A little more than I'd like."

An ambulance screamed out of Banner Hospital. Layton braked and let it pass.

"When you pull into Circle K," the man said, "park under a tree."

Layton followed a Cruise America into the parking lot. The RV headed for the pumps. A blonde in a jeans skirt and camisole that showed her tits stood on the island. Her sandals had high wooden heels and leather straps that crisscrossed her calves. What looked like leggings were tattoos. She plunged the windshield squeegee up and down in the water and grabbed a handful of paper towels.

Layton whistled. "Is that your wife?"

"Yeah, that's her."

"She's good looking."

"She's a babe all right."

The blonde sashayed over to the Bronco and flipped back the wipers.

Layton parked nearby. "Want to switch drivers?"

"No, you can drive. We'll just follow. I signed off on the registration already. Tomorrow when you go to the DMV, just give them the plates."

"You'd trust me to do that?"

"Yeah, why wouldn't I trust you?"

"Because you don't know me from Adam."

"I'm a good judge of character." The tattooed man got out of the car. Before closing the back door, he bent to look in. "I find that if you treat people right, they tend to rise to the occasion."

"Hey, wait!" Layton threw the car in park and jumped out. "What about my car? The Alero. How am I supposed to get it home?"

The tattooed man turned. "We live five miles south of here, in the middle of the cotton fields. We can drive you back."

"You'd do that for me?"

"Sure. Why not?"

"I don't know. I just thought…"

"Takes all kinds to make the world the good place it is." Smiling, the tattooed man gave Layton a comradely slap.

Layton staggered momentarily. A simple transaction about a car had turned into a lesson about the way non-Mormons lived. Who would have imagined lives could be so different?

"If you wouldn't mind," Layton said, "after we go to the bank, could we swing by my place so I can leave your car in my carport?"

"That'll work," the tattooed man said. "It'll give us time to get to know each other."

Layton, raising his guard, knew he was being proselytized, but he wasn't sure what, exactly, the guy wanted.

THE MEMORY PALACE

———o———

T HE POOL TABLE glows Technicolor green beneath
a single fluorescent light, and Arlo Pastori racks the balls
in their trianglular corral. Then he upends the chairs and push-
brooms the gnawed chicken bones and cold fries. In the slop
sink near the johns, he fills the mop bucket. Bracing himself for
the screech of rusty wheels, he pushes the soapy, steaming water
toward the tavern's door. Arlo feels like putting some muscle
behind the mop, his only exercise after a morning in the ER,
and he settles into a steady, swiping rhythm, the first time he
has felt truly calm all day.

The time between midnight and one is where he slips up,
and because of that, Arlo needs to establish a routine. His
support group says it would be good for him, and he knows
it's true; also, that he thinks too much, often to his own det-
riment.

His back is turned when the door brushes the wind chimes.
A man, sagging like a melting snowman, momentarily pauses, holds a foot suspended above the floor, then, making up
his mind that it's not too late to interrupt an employee who's
obviously closing up, steps onto the wet swirls and blinks
through fogged glasses at the pool table, dartboard, and TV.

The man wears a long, woolen coat and brown felt fedora. It takes Arlo a moment to put the face and name together.

Arlo uses a technique called The Memory Palace to keep his regulars' names, jobs, and drink preferences in order. He learned about The Memory Palace from a guy on YouTube who'd won big on *Jeopardy*. What it all boils down to is this: You make a dollhouse in your mind and furnish it with things the customer might have in his or her real home. In a sense, Mazetti's — this tavern in East Liberty, Pennsylvania — is their real home. It's men like this guy — *Brian*. That's it. — who allow Arlo to keep up his car payments and pay his rent.

"Closing early?" Brian says.

Arlo kicks aside the bucket. "Not for another hour."

Brian removes his hat and earmuffs. He takes his time unwinding a hand-knit scarf and hanging his coat on a peg. Summer and winter, the worn sleeves of long johns protrude from beneath whatever shirt he wears on top, tee shirts in the summer, flannel when the snow begins to spit. He works construction. Carpenter, originally. Foreman now. Brian's room in The Memory Palace is furnished with his-and-hers Barcaloungers, a bottle of Dewar's, a red metal Sears toolbox, and the Pittsburgh Penguins on a Samsung 42-inch flat-screen TV — a birthday gift to himself. The steel-toed work boots give him a lumbering, robotic stride, but he's not weaving or putting out a hand to steady himself on the bar. Arlo won't have to decide when enough is enough or whether to call the cops, something he has never done for a regular. He'd rather put them in a cab.

Brian settles onto a stool.

Arlo ducks under the bar and ties on an apron. "The usual?"

"Not tonight." Brian's fleeting smile turns upside down.

"What'll it be, then?" Arlo says.

"Nothing with sugar."

"Diet Sprite okay?"

"Sure. I guess."

Arlo has already scooped up ice, but he puts down the soda gun. "Rather have coffee?"

"No coffee."

"Can't sleep?"

"Not much."

Brian used to come in with his wife. They'd have a double order of wings and fries, with Brian scarfing down the lion's share. As far as Arlo knows, Brian's wife hasn't died or divorced him. East Liberty is a small enough place that word gets around.

Arlo takes this no-sugar, no-caffeine thing to mean that Brian is depressed.

"Missus on your case about something?"

"Not really."

Arlo stops wiping the counter. Brian stares into his drink.

"You know that Tom guy?" Arlo asks, trying to make conversation. In The Memory Palace, Tom occupies the room next to Brian's. "Snowplow driver?"

"I guess."

"I've seen you shoot pool with him."

"I know who you mean."

"He dropped fifty pounds."

"Good for him."

"Of course, he's got motivation."

"Why's that?"

"Wife's seeing someone else."

"Is he aware of that?"

"She put him on notice."

"That's not a surprise. He's a number one a-hole."

Behind Brian's glasses, Arlo sees Brian's rheumy eyes, but figures Brian doesn't really mean to come off negative. The psych prof at community college says copping an attitude is a sign of depression and that depression is a sign of anger turned inward and that all of this stems from childhood. Yadda, yadda, yadda; but it seems to make sense.

"Tom had a heart attack a month ago," Arlo adds.

"You don't say."

"Guy your age," which Arlo assumes to be mid-fifties.

Brian picks out an ice cube and hockey-pucks it down the counter. "What do I owe you?"

"Three bucks."

"For a soda?"

"I asked what you wanted."

"For a buck more, I could have had a shot."

"Hey. You came in. You got warm. You took up a stool."

"Don't get all bent out of shape." Brian fishes out a worn leather wallet and puts money on the counter. He slides a foot to the floor.

"You're not broke are you?" Arlo said.

"It's not the same is all. I mean, value-wise."

"If you want value, you can go over to 7-Eleven and buy a can. I'm sure they'd be happy to rent you out their curb, even if it is twenty degrees and midnight."

Brian resumes his perch on the stool. "At least I wouldn't have to listen to advice."

Arlo looks down the counter. The ice cube has left a trail. The boss man doesn't like coming in and seeing a splotchy counter. Arlo attacks the streak with his counter rag. "I wasn't offering advice."

"You were making inquiries. Advice comes next."

With the flat of his hand, Arlo corks the pinot and merlot. "I'm just being friendly, like they taught in bartender school."

"You should go back to school."

"My mom's always telling me that."

"Why don't you? You're young enough."

"I make better money doing this."

"It all comes down to money, doesn't it?"

"Indeed, it does." Already, he knows Brian isn't going to tip him. Plus, he still has to finish mopping the floor. He ducks under the counter, walks over to the entrance, flips the sign on the door from OPEN to CLOSED, and turns off the blinking neon Coors' sign.

Ignoring the hint, Brian raps the bar with his knuckles. "I think I'll have another."

"Another soda?"

"The soda kind of made me want to puke."

"I thought so."

"You thought what?"

"Willpower only goes so far."

"I don't have a drinking problem."

"Sure, bud. Whatever you say."

After ducking under the bar again, Arlo fishes out a glass from the tepid dishwater. He doesn't bother rinsing the glass, just dries it thoroughly and cleans ChapStick from the rim. He turns and looks at the glass shelves, wiped down with Windex once a month, the mirror behind them washed every six. He's worked his way up to head bartender, and it's his job to keep the place spic-and-span.

He reaches for a bottle. "Dewar's this time?"

"No, let's try a Glenlivet, just for grins."

"The high-priced spread."

"Yeah, well, I'm limiting myself to one, so might as well make the most of it."

The Memory Palace says Brian ought to be asking for a Dewar's white label. Arlo supposes he can revise his picture, but he's never tried that, and he's afraid the new picture wouldn't stick.

"Here you go." Arlo sets the glass down hard. "One Glenlivet on the rocks."

"I didn't say anything about ice, did I?"

"I'm sorry. I just took for granted—"

"If I wanted ice, I would have said ice."

"Want me to dump it?"

"What I was getting at was, you pay for the good stuff, you don't want it diluted. You want to see it coating the side of the glass."

Arlo replays what Brian has told him up to this point, and figures this isn't about the job or the wife at all. Averting his eyes, he serves up a double.

"Here you go."

"Hey, hey. I didn't ask for that."

"On the house." Arlo reaches for the glass with ice.

"No, leave it." Brian caps the glass with his palm. "If it's watered, it's not as hard on your stomach."

"Who told you that?"

"My doc." Brian swirls the new glass and holds it to the light.

"What's the deal?"

"Ah, nothing to get excited about. Just an upset stomach."

"Touch of flu?"

"Doc says blood count's on the low side."

"What's that have to do with your stomach?"

"Doc says my stomach might be bleeding, but you know how they are. They want you to come in for tests and more tests, and all of it costs money, so I basically figure if he can't tell what's wrong with a stethoscope and poking around with his cold fingers, then it's nothing to worry about."

The mop is leaning against the wall. The clock reads twelve-thirty. Arlo has been trying to leave promptly at one, with no dawdling. The people at his meeting say that as the child of a drinker, he has control issues, making too many adjustments, anticipating requests before they're even made. His breath comes fast, as if he is already outside in the sleet, his collar turned up against the cold, East Liberty's gangbangers shoving him left and right until his resistance suddenly breaks and he walks them to the nearest ATM. Better to give them money than eat a knuckle sandwich. He also tends to imagine the worst.

"So, what are you planning to do about your stomach?"

"Just wait it out."

"Are you in pain?"

Brian swigs his drink. "This helps."

"If you're done, I'll wash that."

"Yeah, I'm done."

Arlo wipes off the lip print. "You know what they told my mom?"

"No, what?"

"It would be cheaper if she bought a gun and blew her brains out."

"Who told her that?"

"Her doctor."

"Why'd he say that?"

"She started bleeding from her stomach. Abdomen cramped up all the time. Shitting blood. She kept telling us she had a tape worm."

"That's funny."

"Very funny. Especially when it's your mom."

"I'm sorry. I didn't mean it that way."

"She's in the hospital. I gotta go see her tomorrow and bring her a nightie."

"She have insurance?"

"You kidding?"

"Who's paying for it?"

"Me and my brothers. Or, your tax dollars if we can't come up with a payment plan."

"What'd they do to her?"

"Gave her a couple pints of blood for starters and looked at her stomach with a fiber-optic probe."

"Did they see anything?"

"A hole the size of a pencil eraser. Blood was leaking from her stomach lining into her abdomen."

"Man!"

"I know. It's bad."

Brian slides off his stool. He plants his feet wide and sways like a football center getting ready to bend down and hike the ball.

"How long are they keeping her in?" Brain says.

"I don't know."

"And when she gets out?"

"I don't know." His mom doesn't occupy a room in the Memory Palace. She lives in a dank little studio behind a liquor store. Tomorrow he has to deal with her cats. That's as far as he's gotten with the future.

"Never go to the hospital," Brian says. "That's my motto. Hospitals make you sick."

"You want one more?"

"I should go. See if the wife's still up."

Brian puts a twenty on the bar. Arlo hands him a ten and two ones. Brian peels off a one. "Here you go."

"Thanks, man." Arlo lifts the cash box from the register. That untouched drink is sitting right between them, the dissolving ice floating on top. He should throw it out, throw it out right this second, because otherwise, the instant the door closes, he's going to slug it down. He knows he will. It is not a decision, so much as a surrender.

"There's this meeting over at the Presbyterian Church," Brian says.

"I'm aware."

"Thought I saw you. A month back?"

"You go there?"

"Now and then. When I don't have something better to do."

"Why'd you mention it, then, if you aren't really going?"

"We were talking about your mom."

"Yeah. Well. She won't go."

"Maybe this time'll be different. She had a scare."

Arlo looks at the glass. Brian does the same.

"One can always hope," Arlo says.

"One can always hope."

As Brian, rebundled, steps through the door, the wind chimes accompany his departure.

Arlo picks up the glass and dumps it down the drain. It's a shame to waste good whiskey, but Glenlivet's not his drink. Besides, Brian already called dibs.

The bottle's in his room. Might as well leave it there.

ALL I HAVE

———◦———

W HEN I HEAR the sneaker land softly on the sidewalk, I look back, past the deep shadow of recessed doorways, past the alley, to the pools of light illuminating the weeds. Hurrying toward the next streetlamp, I listen for another footfall. I hear it again and turn. This time I see him, a man with an eagle nose, sharp chin, and wary eyes. He has on a White Sox baseball cap. His hands are spread firmly inside his jacket pockets as if he is containing his very guts. I fix these details in my mind because witness testimony is notoriously unreliable, and I wouldn't want the police arresting a man simply because of his skin color. Did I mention he's black?

With his bouncy steps and long stride, the man is gaining on me, but seems more interested in the demolition of the old brick library we're walking past. His eyes fasten on a construction crane. Its boom is tilted like a fractured bone, and the streetlights reflect off the steel ball dangling ten stories above the sidewalk. He passes me, and then looks my way and points.

"That thang," he says, "could drop down and hit us."

Us. Me and him. We die together.

"Splat." His hands zigzag like an umpire signaling safe at first. Only not safe. More like flattened.

My fingers curl around the purse in my right hand. In my left, I grip a heavy tote bag of books, getting ready to swat him if I have to.

He slows his pace and walks a yard to my left. "Got balmy all of a sudden."

Should I talk to him or not? He could be crazy. He could be homeless. I can't tell. Crazy people can be violent, but the homeless don't generally hurt people; on the other hand they can be overly aggressive. Whenever I'm annoyed by their begging, I remind myself that without dad's paycheck I'd be on the streets, too.

My big challenge right this moment is to feel emboldened, like it's my right to walk around in the world. For a sec there, the sizzle on the back of my neck made me want to run, but the feeling has gone away. Something about the man's walk reminds me of a little kid trying to act perky, even though he's scared to death of the dark. Whistling in the graveyard.

He stops at a light. "Not going to be warm 'bout three o'clock in the morning."

Here comes the pitch, I think. Next, he'll ask for spare change. He's cold. He's hungry. He's whatever.

I pause on the curb, ready to cross to the parking lot. The lot has an attendant, but my car is six stories up, and I don't want this man following me. Then, I see that he has moved away and is cutting across a corner park, heading elsewhere.

A second before he disappears, I turn, as if I had meant to speak to him all along. "Why are you worried about three o'clock?"

He stops, ear cocked in my direction. "You talking to me?"

"Yes, I was." The corner is well lit. People are coming out of an athletic club across the street. If need be, I can yell. "Do you have a place to stay tonight?"

"No ma'am." He turns and comes back to the corner. "Looks like I gotta walk 'round tonight."

"I thought there was a shelter in Evanston."

"That's where I be going. But they give me a date two weeks down the line."

"You mean they're full?"

"Yes, ma'am. They full up." He drawls his vowels like he was brought up in the South, or maybe just the South Side, down in the projects. He turns his head from side to side, as if he looking for a new opportunity to get his life on a better track.

"I guess you don't have a permanent address," I say.

"You got that right."

We stand face to face. He has gaunt cheeks, graying sideburns, and a beak of a nose. He is nodding and rocking back and forth on his heels and biting his lips.

SIX MONTHS AGO, I wanted to get rid of my body. Lights out. Theater dark. For fear of a kid finding me, I decided against a park. The library was a place I liked to go, and the tile floors would have been easy to clean up. My thought was that a librarian would find me and know what to do. Besides doctors, who go to school forever and then lord it over people who haven't, librarians are the most competent people I know. On the day I decided to do it, the library locked its doors, and so I had to resort to home.

I feel a hand on my arm.

"Excuse me, girl," the man says. "You zoned out on me."

"I'm back." I am trying so hard to stay in this place, stay in this life, but, sometimes, it feels like I might just melt down into a puddle, like the Wicked Witch of the West. The crosswalk sign switched from WALK to DON'T WALK.

"I call myself a optimistic kinda man, but I be acting more chipper than I feel inside. Know what I mean?"

"I sometimes feel that way, too," I say, wanting to keep a little edge on him by not admitting that I feel that way all the time, that if my folks had any idea how often I thought about giving it a second try, I'd be back in the day room weaving baskets.

"So I be saying to myself, don't do nothin' desperate now. Know what I mean?"

"Sure enough," I say. He has this mannerism, like a Baptist preacher coaxing "Amens" out of the congregation.

"See, I just got out of jail tonight." He fishes in his pocket and pulls out a ziplock bag of pills.

Oh, great. A criminal. And drugs, too.

"I'm a epileptic, and they give me just nine pills. I got me a prescription, but I been both to Evanston Hospital and the emergency room at St. Francis, and they telling me I got to pay for the pills. When I got out of jail, I went back to the place I was staying, and my old lady had left with all my stuff. I been going all over town trying to get this prescription filled and look like nobody want to help me."

I tuck my purse under my arm, turn my wrists inside out, and hold them under the streetlight.

He looks at the scars, thrusts out his lip, and nods. "Then you know what I'm talking about. They say I got to be having a fit before they can help me. Can I get to the hospital if I be having a fit?"

"Listen," I said, "you could just go sit in the emergency room and wait. Don't take your medicine. Let it come on. I did that once, stopped taking the meds —"

"They used to give me phenobarbital, but I don't have to explain it to you. You know about the medication."

"They gave me that once," I say. "Turned me into a zombie."

"You know you got to have an address, or you can't get no public aid?" the man said.

"I'm not on public aid," I say.

"How you get your meds?"

"My parents," I say, "but I'm about to go off their plan. Then, I don't know. Maybe I'll go cold turkey."

"You a white girl, but look like don't nobody want to help you neither. Bureaucratic. Is that the right word?"

"Bureaucratic mumbo jumbo," I say, thinking of the doctors and how they didn't want to let me out. One said I wasn't well enough. Another said he thought I was okay, as long as my folks kept an eye on me.

"I gone over to the Osco." He waves to the drug store around the corner as if it's on the other side of the earth. "And they tell me it's going to cost $12.95 to get this prescription filled." He turns the pockets of his jeans inside out, takes a wadded-up aluminum wrapper from a pack of gum, and throws it on the ground.

I scoop it up. Litterbugs bother me.

"You shouldn't just throw stuff on the street," I say. "What'd you do that for?"

He fishes a hand in his jacket pocket and holds six pennies in his palm. "This be all I got to my name."

"Does that make it okay to throw trash on the street?"

He snorts disgust. "That's harsh."

"What's keeping you from living with your family?"

"They don't want nothing to do with me."

"Yeah, after a while you don't want to impose." One of the patients I got to know in the day room told me he could get out, but he decided to stay in for a while. He couldn't face going back until he got his life together.

"They's people out here on the streets who is just plain poor," the man says. "Oh sure, they's your drug addicts and your crazies, but lots of folks are just down on their luck."

"I'm one of the crazies," I say, "but I don't live on the street.

Not yet."

He looks me up and down, then rears back laughing. "You not crazy, honey. You just young."

I have this urge to tell him I did drugs, drugs that made my skin itch so bad I thought bugs were eating me up. I have the urge to tell him how I stole from my parents and sisters and how my dad's lawyer got me off the time Nieman Marcus caught me shoplifting. Meth made my brain as empty as this man's pockets. I want to tell him so bad I ache from keeping it in. I can feel the truth in my throat, almost choking me, but that is what my parents made me promise — *Keep it a secret*, they said. *You have your whole life ahead.*

I understand this beak-nosed man. His hands are slipping off the end of the rope. Thinking about his fits coming back makes him reckless. He thinks he has nothing left to lose. But he does. He could lose his last chance.

I put my bag of books on the sidewalk and reach in my purse. I keep back two dollars for the parking attendant and hand over two tens and six ones. If I had more, I would press him to take it. He is the first person in years, maybe ever, who makes me feel connected to the human race. He talks to me like someone who's going through what he's going through, not like a girl about to fuck up again.

He smooths out the bills. Then he pinches each one between his thumb and forefinger and counts them. "Lady, I don't know what to think about this."

"It's not much, but it's all I have."

"I can get my prescription filled and get me a bite of something warm."

"Well, then, good luck."

"Wouldn't be right for me to hug you, would it?"

He looks scared now. He wants to. But he doesn't want to offend me.

I smile for the first time in days. "It would be all right for you to hug me."

As he wraps his arms around me, his cheek brushes mine. He is a good hugger and holds me right up against his body for a long moment.

Then his body goes rigid. His arm becomes a vise around me. I try to draw back to see his eyes because maybe he is having a fit and I'll have to perform some heroic action, like press his tongue with a spoon to keep him from swallowing it. Even though I push, I can't get free of his arms, can't see anything but his jacket collar.

Then he lets go and falls. My arms are free and there is no one to hang onto. Thank God for 911.

Kneeling, a hand on his shoulder, I roll him onto his side and listen for a siren. My fingers, trying to calm his spasmodic jerking and the manic ticking of his heart, stroke his arm. Poor man. For some of us, just continuing to exist is unbelievably hard.

He can't see that he has everything to live for and nowhere left to go but down.

BODY LANGUAGE

———o———

B ECAUSE THIS IS something Mother needs to hear,
I tell her it's good to be home. The bay window, large
enough to accommodate two wingback chairs, looks out on
Lake Michigan. The boat dock has rotted, but Mother thinks
it's not worth repairing because no one sails anymore. Even so,
that stretch of slate-gray water reminds me of the beauty and
vastness of this earth. The lake is as large as some seas. A walk
along the beach, or even better, a moment watching the sun
hover at the horizon, is the closest to heaven I expect to ever
get.

We're each seated in a wingback, and on the octagonal table
between us sit two shirt boxes. They are tied with ribbons, one
red and one yellow, the color of the roses I wear on Mother's
Day, one for this, my living mother, and one in remembrance of
the mother I did not find until she was dead.

"Before we start in about Danny," Mother says, "is there
anything you want from the house?"

She thrusts a clipboard toward me and folds her age-freck-
led hands.

A pen dangles from the clipboard.

An inventory sheet lists the sterling silver, china and crystal, my canopy bed and hope chest, and my father's 1766 Charleville Musket, once owned by Lafayette. There's also my dad's mechanical piggy bank, a first edition of Darwin's *Origin of the Species*, two Elsa Schiaparelli necklaces, a Handel floor lamp, Danny's Jetson's lunch box, our old family VHS tapes, my old Greenleaf Arthur dollhouse and all its furnishings, plus pages and pages more.

"This must have taken you forever to compile," I say.

She shrugs. "I hired an estate agent."

I strike a line across the page. "Sell it." I hand back the clipboard.

She takes it, not even blinking at my gesture. "Don't you want *anything?*"

"You've seen Mexico. Nothing's formal. I practically live on the patio."

"Is everything set?"

"It is."

"Will I like it?"

"The *casita?* Yes, and my house is just steps away."

"I don't want to be a burden."

"Of course not. You won't be."

On the limestone mantel sits a gold, ormolu clock flanked by crystal sconces with small, yellowed shades. A collector, she made sure she had one of everything in this house. One boy. One girl. She rescued me from the scrapheap of orphandom more than fifty years ago. The weight of what I owe her is almost too great to bear.

"You say you found Danny," I said.

"I found out *about* him. Not him, *per se.*"

"Did you hire a detective?"

"No."

"You could have," I say. "Money being no object."

Her bottom lip pushes up and trembles. She's so tiny and fragile. Her feet barely touch the floor.

"Is there some big secret you couldn't tell me over the phone?"

Again, that trembling lip.

Scenarios of Danny's self-destruction turn in my mind. Was it murder or suicide, drugs or alcohol?

"Well?"

Mother takes a folded paper from her pocket. "This came from Social Security." She holds it out.

I read the letter. Danny has been hit by a car. Then I read the date. He has been dead two years. *Two years?*

"Why didn't Social Security notify you sooner?"

"I want you to go out to San Diego and find out," she says.

"No way," I said. "Danny used up every bit of my goodwill, and I didn't have much to start with."

Her chin puckers and she turns toward the sideboard. We all have ways of numbing ourselves. Armagnac is Mother's anesthetic *au choix.*

"Shall I pour you a drink?" I say.

She turns back. "I always wait until four o'clock."

It's three-thirty. Four is her line in the sand.

"Wouldn't you rather I spend the time with you? We could drive down to the Art Institute, or maybe there's an exhibit at the Field. I wager you haven't been there in years."

"Not since Danny was a boy." Her knotty fingers come toward me, and though I owe her, I cannot bear her touch. I spring up and move to the window. On my refrigerator in Mexico I have a magnet that reads, *I have one nerve left, and you're standing on it.*

Out in the lake, sails luff in the wind, and close to shore a man on a sailboard struggles to stay upright.

"Is your time so precious?" she says.

"Not really."

"Sunny, I need your help."

72

How little she has ever asked of me.

"All right, Mother. Of course, I'll go."

"Thank heaven." She sighs and folds her hands in her lap.

"But I'm not optimistic about turning up anything new."

"You found your birth mother."

I smiled. "True. Quite the needle in a haystack."

"But you did it."

"Apart from whatever I have going on genetically, I have one personality trait I definitely get from you."

"What's that?"

"Once we make up our minds to do something, we see it through to the end."

"Just so." She lifts the boxes from the table and places them on her knees. "Now, about the boxes. One is Danny's and one's yours."

"What's in them?"

"Your childhood," she says.

I shake the boxes. Something rattles.

"Don't open them now," she says. "Call a cab and go straight to the airport. You'll have time to go through them in San Diego."

"But I haven't even unpacked!"

"No need to," she says. "You're getting on a plane."

Diminutive though she is, there's no sense arguing with Mother. Flying back across the continent seems a fool's errand; however, I understand that this search is as important to her as finding my birth mother was to me. When I searched for her, I spent years reading through the "chattel sales" in the official notices of Chicago papers. My mother didn't know my birth mother's name, only that she had grown up in Kansas City and hid out in a home for unwed mothers on the North Shore. The Cradle, it was called. Both Danny and I came from there, but he never bothered to search.

Mother must want to close out Danny's trust fund before she joins me in Puerto Vallarta. I know she's going to love it there. The balmy winters. The expat community, many of whom are energetic seniors and as passionate about bridge as she is. The one thing holding her here was the hope that Danny would finally come home.

MOTHER'S LAWYER DRAFTED a power of attorney so that I can act on her behalf, and when I arrive at the hotel in San Diego, I pull a steno pad from my carry-on. I'm hoping the authorities here won't tell me I need a California lawyer as well.

In the morning I'm up early (the time difference helps). I get myself organized: addresses for the pertinent offices; coffee from the Westin's lobby. During my years of searching, I became quite adept at leaping over roadblocks and piecing together the puzzle of a nameless person who seemed to have vanished without a trace. With Danny, I have the advantage of knowing a name and a place of death.

In the San Diego County Recorder's office, I can't help but feel a pang of loss when I read his death certificate. The immediate cause, impact of a motor vehicle. The proximate cause, severe internal trauma.

Severe internal trauma would pretty much describe Danny's entire life. The internal trauma of being adopted. The knot in the pit of his stomach. The inchoate rage against our adoptive parents. But I still cannot see him hit by a car. Dead of a drug overdose or killed in a bar room brawl, yes; but not dead of something as irrelevant and ordinary as getting struck by an automobile.

Since the Social Security office opened up this whole inquiry, I go there and take a number. The indigent, people in old clothes and shoes separating from the soles, remind me that poverty of the spirit is as much a problem as physical poverty.

Slouched in their chairs and waiting for their numbers to be called, the supplicants make nervous, hand-wringing gestures. Their body language tells me that life has beaten them down and left them with only their trembling anxiety, which might either be classified as paranoia or a clear-sighted recognition that the maze of life has only a single exit—death.

At some point Danny would have been sitting in one of these chairs and holding a number. Waiting to get on the dole. What I don't understand is how he could collect Social Security when he'd never worked an honest day in his life. Of course, neither have I. But then, I can live on Father's trust fund. Father's will stipulated that until Danny cleaned up his act, the executor at the bank could not let Danny touch the money.

The psychologists, addiction experts, and social workers all said Danny had to hit bottom. Never send money, they said, as that was the worst thing, and he would only use it to further his self-destructive behavior. My father thought Danny's real parents must be criminals and drug users. That's what we talked about back then, back when I was the overachiever, the good adoptee. The "real parents" versus the "adoptive parents." Danny's therapists said he was caught in a tug-of-war between nature and nurture and had chosen to act out.

We all had roles in this psychodrama. Mother was the "enabler." I was the "codependent." Father, by the time he pulled himself away from the Board of Trade and involved himself in the nitty-gritty of Danny's addiction and attempts to break away from it, was told that he had to "establish boundaries." A banty rooster of a man trying to enforce boundaries on a son two feet taller. Even now, thinking about their futile, unending fights leaves me exhausted.

A heavyset woman with persimmon lips introduces herself as Mrs. Walker and hip-bumps the air as she escorts me to her cubicle. Tacked to the walls are pictures. The young women showing off their babies look just like her, contented and fat.

Mrs. Walker asks why I'm here.

I hand her the letter and power of attorney and say I have some questions.

Reading, her eyes dart back and forth. "Uh-huh. I imagine you do."

Mrs. Walker punches the keys on her word processor to call up Danny's file.

"He started receiving SSI in 1997," she says.

"What's SSI?"

"Social Security for the mentally or physically disabled."

"What were the grounds for his qualification? Alcoholism or drug addiction?"

"I can't say," she tells me. "That would violate his right to privacy."

"But he's dead."

She shakes her head. "Doesn't matter."

"Why did it take two years for you guys to notify us?"

"We only have a part time staffer to locate families of the indigent."

"All they would have had to do is write to his home address."

"He didn't list one."

"What about our parents' names?"

"Nothing."

"Did he list my name?"

Mrs. Walker glances at the screen. "No, he didn't. It was just like he sprang out of thin air."

"In a way he did."

"How so?"

"He was adopted."

"Oh?"

"He was always more at home with his stoner friends than he

was with us."

"Ain't nothing you can do if they want to run with the wrong crowd."

"That's the truth."

This woman confirms everything that I believe. Danny was ultimately responsible for his own fate.

"Where's my brother buried?"

"He was cremated at the expense of the county."

"Can I get his ashes?"

"The crematorium disposed of them."

"What?"

She nods. "The county morgue keeps the body for six months, then they're required by state law—"

"My brother vanished in a puff of smoke?" Saying that out loud sounds ludicrous. "I'm not trying to be funny."

"I know, honey. You wouldn't believe how many homeless pass over, and nobody claims them."

All the air goes out of me. "How are families supposed to have closure?"

"I know where you're comin' from." Mrs. Walker hands me a tissue and then writes a phone number on a Post-it. "There's a police report with details about the accident. Where he was struck and all. That's your next step. At least, you'll have something to tell your mom."

BACK AT THE HOTEL, while I'm waiting for room service to send up a veggie burger, I stare at the Post-it, certain that contacting the police will net me another document like the death certificate: factual, but ultimately not a way to chase down answers. Was he drunk or stoned? On heroin or opiates? Suicidal? Why didn't he just come home? And why does it even matter?

I pour myself a club soda and sit down on the bed, opening Danny's box. Inside is a collection of boy things—rocks, a pocketknife, matchbox cars, a Cub Scout scarf. I can't imagine Mother as a den mother. Maybe she hired someone to do it for her. Where were his Indian headbands and peace signs made of Popsicle sticks? His lanyards? The rubber tourniquets and needles and 'ludes? I pick up some report cards from primary school, curious to read them in light of what he became. "A sweet boy," "artistically gifted," "sensitive and compassionate with other children;" and "Danny certainly knows his dinosaurs!" Beneath these papers are crayon drawings, pictures of soccer camps and classroom photos, and at the very bottom, like an archaeological dig, greeting cards that congratulate the three of us on the adoption.

I was fifteen, and I remember thinking Danny's adoption was exactly like one of mother's shopping trips. She drove down to Evanston and bought a baby. The Cradle was the place where Bob Hope and Liz Taylor got their kids. Mother used to tell people about her six degrees of separation from the movie stars, and also, in a humble-brag, about how much the adoption cost. The price had gone up since the time they got me. I cost $4,500, but for Danny, the boy who was supposed to carry on the Richardson family name, they paid $25,000. What a poor bargain.

A waiter brings my supper, and after I've eaten, I open my box.

"For Sunny, on a Sunny day," a drawing says. "From Danny." All the y's and d's face the wrong way. Danny has me standing on the dock next to my Sunfish, the little sailboat that gave me my nickname. My curly, copper hair blows wildly. He has drawn me with white shorts, and his picture shows blue circles for my eyes. Danny would have been about five or six when he drew this, and I was over twenty, a time I took him sailing nearly every day. He licked his pink bottom lip continuously because the wind dried it out, and he learned the hard way to duck the boom as we came about. I remember holding his head against my breast and pressing a cold rag against the lump.

I lift and unfold a map of the world from the box. It had once hung on a bulletin board above my bed. I spread it on the table and move my index finger across countries whose names have changed, borders that no longer exist. I can almost see Danny's index finger following mine, his lips working earnestly at Madagascar and Zanzibar and Dar es Salaam.

This is wiping me out. I can do no more today.

THE NEXT MORNING, before heading to the police station, I call ahead so they can locate the record of the accident. By the time I arrive, eleven o'clock, Sergeant Ford, an officer in a Charlie Chaplin mustache, has found the file and offers his condolences. He's as tall as Dan — 6'5" — but the vest bulks him up and makes him even more imposing. On the way to a conference room, he offers coffee. I say thanks, but I just want to know what's in Danny's file. Anything he can tell me about my brother's death would be welcome.

He grabs coffee for himself and then sits down and stirs in creamer with a wooden swizzle stick.

His eyes move down the page. "Your brother was busted a couple of times for vagrancy."

"That's it?"

"Should there be more?"

"He did time in Folsom."

"When was he paroled?" the officer asks.

"I don't remember."

He turns a page. His eyes run down it. "This is all about the accident." He takes a long drink of his coffee. "As far as San Diego County is concerned, your brother was a model citizen. We've got troublemakers here, but he wasn't one of them."

"Is it possible he was just never caught?"

"Possible, but not likely."

"I turned my brother in for dealing heroin."

The officer looks down and takes a slurp of coffee.

"I did it for his own good."

"Prison can often harm the prisoner, making matters worse."

"Criminals have choices like anybody else." My hands shake with fury. Self-righteousness or guilt? I capture them between my knees.

He flips to the next page and skims its contents. "How much do you know about your brother's death?"

"Nothing," I say.

He scoots a box of Kleenex across the table.

"I'm fine," I say.

He looks at me.

"Really," I insist.

"You might not be when you read this. Your brother was hit by a car while crossing the median of an eight-lane freeway, and the driver claimed he didn't see him before impact."

There's a long silence between us, and then I ask, "Can I have a moment alone?"

"Sure." He slugs down the rest of his coffee, leaves the room, and closes the door.

I skim five pages of barely legible handwriting. Where do cops learn to write? Same penmanship school as doctors, I think. The report lists times and locations and distance from impact. There was a red Jaguar. The driver thought he had hit a deer.

Danny wasn't a real person to the officer who wrote about his death — he was a body in the road — and I am starting to feel hot and dizzy. No breakfast and too much coffee. Acid burns the back of my throat.

When Sergeant Ford returns, I point to two capital B's. "What's this mean?"

"Black's Beach."

"Was he going to the beach?"

The officer laughed. "Black's Beach is a nude gay beach."

"Danny wasn't gay."

"Suit yourself."

I begin to rise from the chair. "He would have killed a man rather than —"

"Calm down."

"I'm calm. I'm just telling you what I know."

"Okay, so he wasn't gay. Homeless men make camps down there, too. We try to roust them out because the nudists complain, but they always go back."

"Would someone remember him?"

"We have so many transients, anyone who might have known him is likely long gone."

"There's one other thing that puzzles me," I say. "The report says he had towels on his feet. Why would that be?"

"Got me. You'll probably never know for sure."

He is wrong about that.

The thing about the towels is one piece of information Mother needs to know. Otherwise, it will just eat at her and give her no rest. I go back to the hotel and lie down. By the time I order up an omelet, take a Prilosec, and change into a sundress, it's two o'clock. Before, I was gathering information. Now, I'm on a mission.

BLACK'S BEACH IS marked by a tiny sign and an unpaved parking lot. On the bluff stands a wooden building, a hangglider port. Gusts of wind whip my skirt and hit my chest like a giant warning hand. *Go back! Go back!* Nevertheless, I step across a concrete barricade and go right to the edge.

Far below, people as small as peanuts lie on towels. The receding tide has left a tangle of kelp, and the damp salty air smells like mildewed sheets. A flapping noise above my head makes me start. A man hovers above me. His feet look close enough to touch.

"I didn't mean to scare you," the man calls down from his swinging perch, "but unless you have a death wish, you should move back from the edge."

He's dressed in a red jumpsuit and harnessed like a baby in a swing. The inflated double-wings of his glider carry him out over the water.

I retreat to the parking lot. Short of jumping off the cliff, how do people get down to the beach?

Boogieboards under their arms, two young men in swimsuits bound past me and vanish over the side of the cliff. I follow and see a vertical trail descending a gully. My sundress and sandals are totally impractical — I should have worn jeans — but if I'm going to find answers, there's only one way to get them.

I brace my bottom leg and let myself slide. Bushes with blood-red bark have a tenuous grip on the rocky soil. I grab one and it slices my hand.

JOGGING ALONG THE firm sand at water's edge, a bearded man wears only a black turtleneck. A naked woman with pendulous breasts and a tiny red bucket walks with her naked son. Three military men in wet jockey shorts and buzz cuts toss a Frisbee. Everything is jiggling! What a freak show.

Father used to say, "Tilt the continent, and the nuts roll west." He hated all that California represented: its liberal politics; its permissiveness; its lure for young men of a certain nature, boys who might have been groomed to be productive members of society had they not slid down the economic ladder and been content to wallow in mire.

I stop to ask a man lying stomach down (thank God) on his towel if he knows of any homeless encampments nearby.

"Ask those guys." He points a lean arm toward a blue tent about fifty yards away. Near it three naked men sit on drift-wood logs. They look like a bunch of nudists with a tent to keep them from getting baked.

Just the same, I walk toward them with my eyes cast down, and when I draw close, I call out, "Do any of you know a Danny Richardson?"

"Who wants to know?"

I look up. "His sister, that's who."

One of the men wears a Dodgers' cap. He is skinny and tan all over, the same color as the cliff. He takes off his cap, and wild, curly hair springs up. He waves the cap like someone try-ing to attract attention in a crowd. "Come on down!"

I take off my sandals. Sand squishes between my toes.

The man in the Dodger's cap stands to shake my hand. "I'm Little Joe."

I show him the reason I refuse the handshake. "A nasty bush sliced my hand."

One of the others — matted dreadlocks; a cave man with a digging stick — says, "Toyons'll do that to you. I'm Paxton. You must be Grace Kelly."

"What the fuck's that supposed to mean?" I say.

"She's got a mouth on her," Paxton says, looking around at the others. "Big Dan never told us Grace had a mouth on her."

"Clothes off?" says the third one. Clean-shaven, with a hel-met of brown hair, he stands, takes his head in his hands, and twists it.

"Don't crack your neck, Bean." Paxton pulls Bean down by the elbow. "It's not good for you."

"Hot." Bean leaps across a log. He clearly is not all there.

I fold my arms across my chest and try to avoid eye contact. These guys scare me a little, but with all the other people pass-ing by, I feel safe enough. "I'm sorry to intrude."

"It's not like we're busy," Paxton says, looking around at the crew.

Little Joe sits. "Bean's just going off to pee. Why don't you take his seat?"

Over by the cliff, Bean stands with his back to us, legs stiff, feet apart.

Wondering what Mother would think if she saw me here, I sit down gingerly on the log.

Paxton leers. "*Mi casa es su casa.*"

"What *casa*?" I ask.

"Be nice, Pax," Little Joe says.

Bean walks toward us. He has the blunt features and elongated arms of a satyr and sits down in the sand next to me, squirming a place for his butt. He obviously has not washed his hands.

"So," Paxton says, "what brings Princess Grace all the way from Chi-ca-ga?"

"My name's not Grace."

Paxton frowns. "It's not?"

"Big Dan always called you Princess Grace," Little Joe says.

Paxton says, "Sorry, but I thought Grace was your name."

"It's Sunny."

Bean tugs at my sundress. "Swim?"

"Don't touch me." I push his hand away.

"Bean had an accident," Little Joe says. "Show your scar, Bean."

Bean drops his head and fans up his shock of hair. A sea worm of a scar starts at his ear.

Little Joe taps his temple. "Bean likes to swim. He wants you to go in the water."

"But I would advise against it." Paxton says. "He'll drown you."

Bean leans away from me, as if he's afraid I'll bully him.

"I came to find out about my brother. Whatever was he doing on a nude beach?"

"Dan never went naked," Little Joe says. "He always wore a swimsuit—"

"—and a warm-up suit," says Paxton, "the color of that tent."

The blue tent nearby sags and inflates with each gust of wind.

"That was Dan's," says Little Joe.

"It's tiny," I say.

"His feet stuck out the end," Paxton says. "But, unlike me, he was religious about his personal modesty. He wouldn't even change his clothes in public."

"How long did he live here?" I ask.

They look at one another.

As in an hourglass, sand runs through Bean's toes.

"Maybe a year?" Paxton says, looking around for confirmation.

"Yeah, he could have been here a year," says Little Joe.

"And before that?" I say.

"Who knows? People come and go," Paxton says.

In the center of the log circle is a fire pit of stones and a cast-iron pot with a domed lid. A blackened saucepan lies upside down in the sand.

"So, what do you guys eat out here?" I say.

"Stale bread. Potatoes. Rice," says Little Joe. "We're having hot dogs for dinner."

"Hot dogs!" Bean smiles.

They probably steal groceries from the nearest store, but still, where is the nearest store? A mile or more away.

"When we get our SSI checks," Paxton says, "we go shopping and buy things on sale." He picks up a clam shell and tosses it my way.

A souvenir. I wipe it off and put it in my pocket.

"Do you have a cooler?"

Paxton says, "We keep cold stuff at Joe's mom's place."

"Velveeta!" says Bean.

"Why don't you just live there?" I say.

"It's a studio," Little Joe says. "And, anyway, I can't stand enclosed spaces."

"Little Joe runs amok if he's confined," Paxton says. "Of course, that's a contradiction in terms."

"Jail," says Bean.

"Oh, yeah. When the cops haul us in on vagrancy, I go ballistic." Little Joe looks out at the ocean. "These guys like jail though. A hot meal and no dishes."

"Big Dan was a real chef," Paxton says. "He had refined tastes."

Bean lifts the lid of the pot. "Chicken."

At this point, it almost seems normal to be looking at their parts, dangling like chicken necks between their thighs.

"If he got a craving, he'd walk all the way to the supermarket —"

" — on those feet," Paxton says.

"What about his feet?" I ask.

"Burning." Bean pokes the cold ash with a stick.

"He was allergic to sand," says Little Joe.

"He had eczema." Paxton scratches a knot of matted hair then examines his fingernails. "The doctor told him he had to stop living on the beach."

"Why would he have towels on his feet?" I ask, remembering the accident report.

"His feet were always swollen. He couldn't fit in his shoes," Little Joe says.

"He was coming back from the hospital," says Paxton.

I look up and down the beach. "What hospital?"

"It's up the hill from here," Joe says. "They'd soaked his feet and wrapped them in towels."

"How do you walk with towels on?"

"They taped them around his ankles," says Paxton. "Did it once a week."

"That's why he got runned over," says Little Joe.

"Run over," Paxton corrects.

"Slippers," Bean says.

"Yeah, big fat slippers." Paxton pulls back his lips, approximating a smile.

"Do you think he could have been trying to commit suicide?"

Paxton snorts. "Are you kidding? Big Dan was one happy camper."

"He'd sit over there by that tent, swig vodka, and smoke. We saved the tent as a memorial. That's a prime spot on the beach."

Little Joe looks out at the water. Across the sky a vapor trail makes a double underscore.

"Tide's coming in," Paxton says.

"Nothing like the blue Pacific," says Joe.

Bean makes a vee with his fingers. "Peace."

I listen to the waves, each crash followed by a kinder swoosh.

I can't help but think that if I'd come two years ago, Danny would have been sitting beside me on this log, his arm touching mine. The last time I saw him he'd grown a Fu Man Chu mustache and acquired eagle-wing tattoos. The left corner of his mouth twitched unless he clamped a toothpick in his teeth to keep it still. He said "deez" and "doze" and called cops "criminals with badges." He wore his hair below his shoulders and dyed it black and sat for hours staring into space. At sixteen, he was raped in county jail—by the guards—and I told him he should stop making stuff up.

Bean reaches in a plastic bag, half-buried in the sand, and pulls out a single hot dog.

"Hey, that's dinner!" Paxton stands and Little Joe grabs the hot dog, holding it while Paxton tackles Bean and throws him to the ground, planting a knee on Bean's chest and slapping his hand. "No! No! No! How many times do I have to tell you!"

"Stop it! You'll hurt him." I leap up and grab Paxton's arm, trying to pull him off. "He's just a boy and doesn't understand."

Bean, sitting up, spits sand.

"You all right, buddy?" Paxton pulls Bean to his feet.

"Swim?" Bean says.

Paxton puts his arm around Bean's shoulder. "Gotta abide by the rules. Right, buddy?"

"Right," Bean says.

Apparently, Paxton wanted to teach Bean a lesson, but what a cruel way to do it.

"Race?" Bean, unfazed, runs for the surf.

"I guess I better. He needs to run off some energy." Sighing, Paxton jogs stiffly before turning to wave. "Goodbye, Princess Grace."

His smile, tense and guarded, reminds me of Mother's.

"I should get going," I say to Little Joe.

"I'll take you up the back way. It's not as steep." Little Joe pulls on a crumpled pair of khaki shorts.

Ice plant — tiny pink flowers and fuzzy, dewdropped leaves — grows beside the dunes. The trail turns into a ladder of crumbling rock. Joe reaches toward my outstretched hand and wraps his fingers around my wrist. I scramble and he pulls. At the top he lets go, but the imprint of his fingers remains. We're both breathing hard.

"Why did Danny call me 'Princess Grace'?"

"He said you looked like her."

"Do I?"

"Personally, I think it's more the *aura of privilege*." He smiles and uses finger quotes.

"Did he hate me?" I'm almost afraid of the answer.

"Dan? No!"

"He sure hated cops," I say.

Little Joe laughed. "The Keystone Kops? Yeah, Dan didn't like his tranquility disturbed."

Far below, Paxton and Bean are starting dinner, and a thread of smoke rises from the fire. A strong gust off the ocean turns the tent into a blue balloon. Anchors pull loose. The sides collapse. A formless blue rag tumbles toward the coiling surf.

I scream for Paxton to run and grab the tent, but Joe puts his hand on my shoulder. "Just let it go."

Of course I should let it go in the broader sense. Maybe I can, but what about Mother? Will she ever let go of her little boy?

Along the horizon an incoming fog bank blurs the boundary between sea and sky. The wind is heavy with damp.

What I can report back to Mother is that the view from the beach matched the view from our dock, a kaleidoscope of the ever-changing sky. Danny made a life near water. We should assume he had been content.

THE BLUE CABOOSE

———○———

SISTER SALINA LIMONE didn't impose her views on other people. That was the fact of the matter, as anyone with half a brain could plainly see. At the end of the day, she came in to find dishes in the kitchen sink. She tidied up. Simple tidying up like any conscientious woman did. And, yes, she had carried Sister Mary Margaret's books and legal pads to the bedroom, but only because the living room, with its old afghan-covered futon and worn overstuffed chair, was where they invited their neighbors — hookers and crackheads and their kids — to stop in for prayers and soup. The children needed an island of sanity, as did she; and even though visiting her father in Colorado might be the Christian thing to do, she didn't think it would necessarily make her a better housemate.

Sister Nearing held up a hand. "Take a breath, Sister Limone."

Salina hopped up. "Can I get you some water?"

"No, thank you," Sister Nearing said with a tinge of impatience.

One of Salina's housemates had stuck a dead palm frond, a remnant of Palm Sunday, in the corner of a framed picture of Jesus, cradling his Sacred Heart. Salina plucked off the frond, crumpled it, and put it in the pocket of her denim skirt. Heavy

90

black gabardine habits hadn't, thankfully, been around for years, and she was glad to concentrate on ministering to the poor, here in this blighted quadrant of northeast Washington D.C.

"Come sit a moment and let's pray." Sister Nearing, the Director of the Mid-Atlantic region, headquartered in Baltimore, patted the futon invitingly.

Salina pulled a chair from the drop-leaf-table. Swinging her leg over the seat, she sat backwards, resting her chin on her clasped hands. "Will you start the prayer, or shall I?"

Sister Nearing rubbed the back of her neck. "Let us be mindful of Our Lord's charity."

Salina sat up straight and closed her eyes. The short pause was abruptly brought to an end by a motorcycle revving in the parking lot. No doubt one of the neighborhood pimps. Meantime, above her head, rhythmic thuds rattled the light. Jorge and his basketball. Salina crossed herself, ending the prayer. There was a time for prayer and a time to be practical, and this was the latter. She had to defend herself against her housemates' accusations.

"The problem's not me," Salina said. "Sister Mary Margaret's not cut out to live with poor folk."

"I hope you're wrong about that."

"I might be wrong about a lot of things, but not about that. She's an intellectual. When she finishes her psych degree, she wants to go teach at a university. Let her. That's what she's called to do. But in the meantime, she's driving me crazy, too. She's always poking around, trying to get me to tell her things that happened in my past. And I don't like it. She doesn't know anything about me, and the more she pries, the less I want her to know. We could live just fine together if she'd pick up after herself."

Salina slid off the chair and went to the window. "I think we need some fresh air."

Pulling back the curtains, she looked out to the parking lot and saw thirteen-year-old Jorge, just beginning to grow a mustache and with a basketball under his arm, hopping on his bike. Opening the door was the signal he could come up for snacks. Apples, oranges, not the things that appealed to him; but sometimes he came up anyway. She opened the door and waited for his footsteps on the metal steps. He didn't come.

"Can't you stop pacing?" inquired the Director.

"I'll try." Salina backed against the wall and crossed her arms. "I'm not pacing. All right?"

"I guess you must be wondering why I drove all this way when a phone call would have sufficed," Sister Nearing said.

"You're going to kick me out."

"Is that why you're so defensive?"

"I have as much right to live here as they do."

"You think I'm going to kick you out?"

"It's two against one."

"Sister Mary Margaret only wants what's best for you."

"I know what's best for me."

Sister Nearing made a steeple of her fingers. "Your repetitive behaviors get on her nerves."

"She tries to mess with my head," Salina said.

"It's not just Mary Margaret." The Director shook her head. "Sister Klanac also finds your behavior annoying."

Fat Sister Klanac? *Lazy* Sister Klanac, the Croatian who didn't eat enough at the bakery where she worked, but had to stick popcorn in the microwave the instant she came home?

"I could complain about her if I wanted," Salina said. "She leaves the lights on. She runs up the electricity."

The Director sighed. "Sister Klanac says you're always jumping up to wipe the counter, even during dinner. If someone drops a fork, you're faster than a busboy."

"It's hard for her to bend over."

"Is that why you get out the dust mop and make a point of

92

dusting around her feet?"

"She's always dropping stuff she can't pick up."

"But you make her nervous," the Director said, her voice rising. "Can't you see that it makes people nervous if you're constantly in motion?"

"I can't help it." Salina turned her back and went out onto the balcony. The parking lot, sadly in need of a truckload of fresh gravel, was full of cars with sagging bumpers and broken windows. Jorge had gone off to the park. She came back in and shut the door.

"Please sit down, Sister." The Director opened her briefcase and removed a manila folder.

"The problem is, I don't like to sit. I was raised to believe idleness is a sin."

"Sit anyway." The Director pulled a handwritten letter from the file. "A year ago you said your father was getting on in years, and at some point, you'd like to take care of him. Has that time come?"

Salina ran her fingers through her close-cropped hair. The last time she'd seen her father, her hair had hung down to her hips. "I didn't say I'd *like* to take care of him. I said I might *have* to."

Standing, the Director put her folder on the chair and reached for Salina's free hand, pulling her away from the wall.

Sister Nearing's fingers felt cold. Her grip tightened. Salina pulled free.

"Perhaps there is some unfinished business," Sister Nearing said, drawing near. "Something in your past?"

Salina took a step back. "There's not." She disliked anyone standing inside the circle she drew around herself, the "hula hoop" she called it.

"A change of scene might do you good."

"Not *that* change of scene."

As far as she was concerned, once a person cut off communication, it was better to keep it cut off. She'd seen her dying clients mend fences with their families, and others try and fail. You could never really fix what had gone wrong in the past. Some things were so broken they could never be mended, and all that Kubler-Ross, death-and-dying talk only led to unrealistic expectations of healing and forgiveness.

Dying people needed their faces washed. They needed their butts wiped. They needed ice chips and swabbed tongues. "Move me someplace else, then," Salina said.

With a sigh of frustration, Sister Nearing returned the folder to her briefcase. "I can't see any other option, Salina. You have to try harder to get along."

"I *try* to get along with people."

"You get along fine with your clients," Sister Nearing said. "It's just your roommates, which I don't really understand because, you know, we've had this conversation before."

Salina hung her head. "Maybe I should never have —"

"No. Don't go there. Let's not question your vocation." Sister Nearing leaned back on the futon and crossed her legs.

Not leaving any time soon, thought Salina. Her skin crawled with ants. She rubbed her arms, not sure how much more of this she could bear.

"It's an odd thing," the Director said. "You don't have a bad temper. You're hardworking and dedicated to the people we're trying to serve. You've found your ministry in home health care. In all these ways the Sisters of Mercy fits you well. For the life of me, I can't figure out what's at the root of your behavior."

"Nothing is at the root of it," Salina said, arms crossed and pacing.

Sister Nearing smiled. "Ever since I met you — how many years ago now? — you've struck me as a very old soul."

"What's that mean?"

"Those black eyes of yours —"

"I'm Mexican!" Salina said.

"Don't take offense."

"I just like to stay busy," Salina said.

"What would you think about if you sat down?" Sister said. "Perhaps there's some, uh, abuse in your background? Something you've been reluctant to share?"

A wave of heat washed over Salina's head, like in the shower, with the water ten degrees too hot. There was no abuse, not sexual, if that's what Sister Nearing meant. And as for how she was raised, well, that was her business. She'd told them all they needed to know.

"What is it you want?" Sister Nearing said.

"I just want everyone to leave me alone."

"Then, go home, Sister Limone."

Banished. Exiled. "For how long?"

"Two weeks, let's say. Better yet, a month?"

"Hospice won't give me that much time off."

"I'll see what I can do."

"But will I have to come back here?"

"I don't have another alternative," Sister Nearing said. "We live in community, Sister Limone."

"I know, I know."

"So, what do you say?"

Two weeks off. Maybe a month. Could she bear it?

"I'm not exactly sure where my father lives."

"What does he do?"

"Odd jobs for ranchers."

"Give me the information, and I'll call the Bishop. Maybe reconnecting with your father will bring you some peace." Sister Nearing rose from the futon, collecting her briefcase.

"I doubt it," Salina said.

"Why's that?" Sister Nearing asked.

"Because I'll have to figure out a place to stay."

"Can't you stay with your father?"

"No," Salina said.

Sister Nearing frowned with concern. "Is he homeless?"

"It's a rural area. Let's just say hogs live better."

"I see," Sister Nearing said. "Well, let's make sure there's someone to meet you. What airport would you fly into? Denver?"

"I'll take the bus," Salina said.

"Are you afraid of flying?"

"I just need time to make a transition."

In parting, Sister Nearing kissed the cross at her neck and took Salina's hands, a goodbye that would have been unthinkable when Salina first joined the order. She bowed her head to show she'd understood and would take the Director's message to heart. If she could.

WEARY FROM THE eighteen-hour trip from Washington D.C., Salina sat near the back of the Greyhound, her parka zipped and hood raised. It was the beginning of May, and traveling back to the high plains of Colorado was like traveling back to winter. Snow covered the Rockies and tears of moisture ran down the fogged windows. She'd managed to sleep through the toilet opening and slamming shut, but as the bus rumbled from town to town, the smell of chemicals had woken her. Now, holding a handkerchief over her nose, she checked her cell phone to see if it had miraculously risen from the dead. A black screen. Not even solitaire. Well, what had she expected, insisting that this was the way she would go home. A bus was safer than hitching a ride, as she had in the old days, so she supposed when she looked at her life in its entirety, this was a step up, though a step she had avoided taking for fear of the memories, not of abuse, but of simple poverty, if poverty, in all its varieties of deprivation, could be called simple.

Fallow fields stretched to the horizon. Some deacon was supposed to meet her. Good thing, too, because without a car, she had no way to get out to where her father lived.

With an ear-popping exhale of hydraulic pressure, the bus braked in the station. Near a line of passengers waiting to board the bus, she saw a man holding a posterboard sign. NUN MOBILE. A white Stetson covered the dome of his head, and he wore cowboy boots and a bolo tie. In all her time out East, she'd forgotten bolo ties.

Last off the bus, she descended the steps.

"I'm your nun," she said, walking up to him. "Sister Salina."

His eyes ran up and down her sweatshirt and jeans. He tipped his hat. "Dr. Francis Clancy, at your service."

"Doctor?"

"Actually, I'm a vet. Large animal. It's 'Doc' to my friends."

"Am I your friend?"

"Sure. Why not?"

The driver had been unloading suitcases from the luggage compartment.

"Which one is yours?" Doc said.

"The pink vinyl."

"The one with Cinderella decals?" He pointed with the posterboard.

"That's the one."

"But it's a kid's suitcase."

"I'm short, and anyway, I found it in an alley."

"Oh-ho! Chip off the old block, I see!"

What was that supposed to mean? She didn't like people who presumed to know her business. The trip had worn her down, and now, on top of seeing her father, she had to deal with this deacon fellow.

He gave the driver a dollar bill and waited in the lobby

while Salina used the restroom. Then he was driving east, and she took out her rosary and fingered the smooth, glass beads. As she knew he would, he took the rosary and the movement of her lips intoning the Our Fathers and Hail Marys as a subtle hint, discouraging small talk. Eventually he took the exit to a state route, and then a county road lined by crooked, wooden fenceposts strung with rusting barbed wire.

The parched grass and clumps of windblown trees signaled yet another rural Colorado town, the one she recognized as her father's mailing address. Passing by the barbershop with its red, white, and blue barber's pole mounted on the wall, she imagined him fortyish, in a worn straw hat, cowboy boots, and ranch jeans — a short, wiry Mexican with a weathered face, thin mustache, and gold tooth. But all these years later, he must have aged. White hair? No teeth? Gray stubble?

The town's small brick post office had a picture window, but its shade was drawn. Somehow she had expected her father to be sitting outside on its empty bench, waiting for her the way he waited to catch a ride with whomever might be heading out to wherever he worked.

Of course, it was possible that the post office had closed permanently. A year ago he'd sent a postcard with the words in Spanish, *No me olvides*, as if pushing him into the darkest corner of her mind could get him to stay there. She had looked up the town on a map and seen that it was like all the places she had grown up: no industry besides ranching and farming, schools barely able to stay open, all the young people fleeing for the cities, the hospitals and government offices closing their doors.

Just after signs for the Elks and Rotary Club — It was seven o'clock by now, and she was hungry and too tired to think about how many hours she'd been awake — the deacon turned into a gravel drive. A hundred feet back from the road sat a white clapboard building the size of a one-room school. Weathered wooden posts held a sign: "St. Mary's Catholic Church."

Stiffly, she got out of the car.

Doc retrieved her suitcase. "Let me show you the church."

"Is my father going to meet us here?"

Doc shot a look at her. In his previous grin, she saw a frown. "But...but, I thought you knew...that's why you've come..."

"What? What should I know?"

Doc removed his Stetson and held it over his heart. "Sister, I'm sorry to have to tell you, your Daddy died two days ago."

The ground fell away. "How could that be?"

"He's been sick for some time."

"With what?"

"Old age."

She looked beyond the church. A few brick houses with small fenced yards sat among the trees. A spotless Airstream gleamed in the light of the rising moon.

Speechless, she stood shaking and hoping the tremble would stop so she could take a step forward. Go see the church, or whatever the deacon expected her to do.

"Now what?"

"There'll be a service. We figured you'd want to plan it."

"Yes, yes, of course," she said. "But I came all this way to see *him*."

"Well, I know he would have been glad to see you, to see any of his kids for that matter. But he understood. Busy with your own lives. My kids are the same way. Scattered all over kingdom come. Happy to let us old duffers fend for ourselves."

"I'm just stunned," she said. "I always thought if he needed me, he would have written."

"He had his pride. Didn't want to bother you. Right at the end, looks like he was trying to put his life in order." The deacon walked to the back door of the church. "See here? Just last week, Hugo put a fresh coat of paint on the church steps."

The deacon took a key from a nail under the top step, and Salina saw that, yes, the back steps were covered with a slick, gray coat of paint, evidence of her father's recent life.

"Where am I to stay?"

"Right here. I made you up a cot."

"Is there a shower?"

"No, but there's running water and a toilet."

The deacon unlocked the back door and led her into a small room that doubled as an office and a dressing room. Below the window was an Army cot, a camping mattress, thread-worn sheets, and folded blankets. A sorry little pillow.

"This be okay?" He spread his arms as if showing her the Taj Mahal.

"I've slept in worse."

The deacon fiddled with the thermostat. A gush of heat came from the floor grate.

Standing in the corner was an old wooden desk of the schoolteacher variety, its desk chair rocked back as if someone had recently been sitting in it. A priest's white chasuble hung in an open wardrobe.

"Who says Mass?" she asked.

"Once a month Father Rodriguez comes out from La Junta."

"La Junta."

"Been there?"

"We lived there."

"It figures."

"What do you mean?"

"There's a lot of Mexicans."

This deacon fellow was getting on her nerves.

"Does Father Rodriguez speak Spanish?"

"Enough to get by."

With a name like Rodriguez, he ought to be fluent. But maybe not. You forgot what you didn't use, and if he was second generation, like her, then chances were good he interacted mostly with Anglos.

The deacon turned on the overhead light. Through the door that opened into the nave, she saw wooden pews, thirty rows in all. This was where her father would have prayed. She slid into the second row and flipped down a kneeler. With its solid clunk on the plank floor came all the inchoate feelings about the way she'd grown up, the things that had propelled her and held her back. Now she understood why her clients were so eager to have that final, deathbed scene. Why they sought forgiveness. Getting it over with. Getting it done. But getting it right most of all.

TWENTY YEARS AGO, her sister, married and with children of her own, had brought their worn-out mother up to Laramie, Wyoming. But their father, always with that far off look in his eyes, had refused to leave this blink-in-the-road he'd decided to call home. Manuela, the sister in Wyoming, didn't want to take him on, and Olga, the next oldest, living in Council Bluffs, said she had her hands full. Juan, the only boy, who lived in a doublewide in San Bernardino, said, "Let him live in one of his crazy little houses." And, so now, Salina guessed, they had all demonstrated their heartlessness and lack of compassion, and the only thing left to do was to pray for the soul of Hugo Limone.

Once again, she slipped her rosary from her pocket and fingered the beads as if she were fingering a rabbit's foot that would ward off the bad luck that had made her arrive too late. If only she had not been so stubborn about taking the bus, she could have seen him one last time. Add that to the list of sins for which she sought forgiveness.

Crossing herself and kissing the crucifix, she sat back in the pew and looked at the tabernacle on the altar. The altar cloth needed starch. Dust lay thick on an antique organ. It had probably been years since anyone played it. Tomorrow, she could clean this all up. She would be burying her father, but also reviving this careworn little church.

Dr. Clancy slid into the pew. She was thinking he'd left unnoticed, but he knelt and bent over, shoulders shaking. Was the kerchief he held to his eyes because he was crying? But, of course, he would be if he and her father had been good friends.

"How, exactly, did he die?"

"Well, ma'am, he laid down in a field and just expired."

"Did he freeze?"

"Not so's the Coroner could tell. Hugo'd put on his Sunday suit —"

She sat back in the pew. "He never had a Sunday suit —"

" — as if he'd a mind to call it quits."

"People don't just die when they want to," she said.

"Horses do," he said. "Why not people, who are supposedly smarter?"

Something was off. "Who's the Coroner?"

"*I* am."

"But don't you have to be a medical doctor?"

"Not here in rural Colorado. It's an elected position." As he looked toward the modest wood crucifix mounted above the altar, his eyes crinkled in a squint. "Anyhow, I looked him over."

She guffawed. "Is this a joke?" she said. "Because the father I remember was quite the practical joker."

He patted her shoulder. "Little lady, I wouldn't pull your leg on something like this."

"I'm still having trouble understanding how he could die. Usually people hang on, even after everyone in their family is more than ready to let them go."

"I reckon that's true."

"Did you tell me what he had? Was it prostate cancer? Leukemia? Pancreatitis? Something painful and untreatable?" A passing truck made the windows rattle. "Otherwise, I don't understand how he could be painting the steps one day, and then just walk out into a field and lie down with the intention to die the next." It was all too impossible. No one *willed* themselves dead.

She took a tissue from her purse and dabbed her eyes, wanting the deacon to think she felt more than she did. Mary Margaret was always probing with her ice pick mind. "Feelings, Sister Salina. What are your *feelings*?" And this was the thing. As she was seeing now for the very first time, she did not have feelings like other people. She pretended to blow her nose. Until she got back to D.C., she'd have to act shaken up, because that was the expected, the natural, reaction.

"It sounds like you knew my father very well," she said.

"Oh, I do." He flinched. "Did."

"How did you even communicate?"

"Pidgin English. What with my two hundred words of horse Spanish and his two hundred words of English, we got on fine. Say, you should take a gander at where your father lived. He's got — had — quite the setup."

"Let me get my bearings first."

"It's only a quarter mile from here, and the walk'll do you good. It's just a shame you got here too late."

Yes, it was. It was ridiculous.

"And wear a jacket," he said. "By the time you walk back, it'll be cold."

"Are you going to come with me?"

"I'll swing back in an hour and round you up for dinner.

THREE CONCRETE SILOS stood like the fortified walls of Italian hill towns, and the train tracks ran past them. At the end of a dead-end spur, she spotted the Atchison, Topeka, and Santa Fe caboose, its paint not red, as she had imagined when Dr. Clancy described it, but the shocking turquoise of the Adriatic Sea. The last time she'd spoken to her father, he'd called from a pay phone. She'd asked him what was new. "Farmers bringing in winter wheat," he'd said in Spanish, but he had never told her about the caboose.

By the time she reached for the steel handgrip and pulled herself onto the rear platform, her teeth chattered and her body ached with fatigue; she could probably have done with a meal. Inside, the beaded wainscoting that came halfway up the walls reminded her of the kitchen in Robert Andresson's house.

A gay man from Abilene, he had shared her love of Fourth of July parades and county fairs; she had walked him through the last six months of his life; and after he had passed, she'd told the order she needed a change and requested a job in a nursing home. Now, here she was dealing with death again, her father's death, when she had not sufficiently grieved Mister Andresson, humorous till the end. Those were the ones it was hardest to let go of, the ones who made you laugh, and she was dismayed to find these heart strings still strumming inside her, the deep ache of loss for a man who was not even a blood relative.

In contrast to the cool sea-blue of the exterior, the entire interior, save for the varnished wood of the wainscoting, was as yellow-golden as dried maize. It was at once cheering and mellowing, and she could easily imagine her father coming in on a cold day and feeling pleased.

On a table flanked by built-in benches sat an open box of Bicycle cards, the jokers set aside, the game of solitaire half-played. She wondered if Dr. Clancy had ever come out here. Surely, if he had, there'd be bottles of bourbon or six packs of beer. In his younger days her father had enjoyed a drink, but never to excess, not like her psychologist roommate seemed to assume.

Opposite the table stood a brown propane stove, a box of matches on the shelf above it. It had been fifty years since she'd seen a stove like that, but she remembered how her grade-school teacher lit it. She knelt and flipped open a door and saw the knob that said, "Pilot." Expecting to blow herself up, she pressed the knob for thirty seconds. The match ignited a blue flame, and by the time the match burnt down to a small black worm, she had the burners on. That'd cut the chill. She would just have a quick look around.

Across from the stove a circular, steel staircase led up to a cupola that she had noticed in a glancing way. Now that she stood inside the caboose, looking up to the second story, a wave of bitterness swept through her, and she crossed herself to make it go away. After all these years her father had found a two-story house for himself. She climbed the stairs. A narrow bench seat had a splendid view of the moonlit snow-covered peaks.

Downstairs, four shallow, workmen's lockers stood on one side of the hall, their narrow doors sticking as she yanked them open. Who was this man, this illiterate sweeper of grain elevators? This church janitor for the little parish of St. Mary's, where the steps and handrail had been carefully brush-stroked gray: his last day's work before his seemingly planned death, about which she had plenty of feelings, mainly shame. And shame for *herself*, it must be said. Not for her blue-collared dad.

HER FATHER HAD been born in Morelia, Mexico in 1920. Twenty-two years later, in 1942, he came north to harvest sugar beets in Stockton, California. He met Salina's mother Lupe, only thirteen, a girl from a family of second-generation field workers. Salina had been told she was named for the Central Valley town that meant "salts". Whomever had registered her birth certificate had dropped the final "s". None of this she'd given a thought to until her father moved them to Colorado. He'd fallen out with a man at work. By then she was in fourth grade, struggling to catch up in math, but a good reader. She had lived on a ranch near Joe's, Colorado for a year. Then, it was six months in Trinidad, six months in Lamar, six months in Cheraw, and finally in La Junta, a town of seven thousand and a place he had attempted to permanently settle.

At fourteen, hoping to get back to the sunshine and warm winters, she'd run away from home, if you could call where they lived "home". She'd fought off a trucker, using the shiv her little brother Juan had given her as a goodbye gift, and the trucker readily dumped her outside Kansas City. After that, she'd taken up with a Southern Baptist short-order cook who'd coaxed her into a full immersion baptism in the Missouri River, and it was the shame of letting herself be brainwashed into joining a congregation that heard voices and rolled on the floor that sent her East. Working in the kitchen at Mercy Hospital in Council Bluffs, Salina spent so many lunch hours in the chapel that Sister Mary Alma, head of Food Services, asked if something was wrong.

"I like to pray," Salina said. Prayer was the only thing that calmed her down.

"Have you ever considered a religious vocation?" Sister Mary Alma said.

"I'm not a virgin," Salina said.

"Your vow of chastity only begins after a period of reflection." Sister Mary Alma had taken her hand, and for the first time since Salina had left home, she felt a slight relaxation of the unkind words she'd called herself for leaving her mother with all those little kids and a quixotic, unreliable jokester of a husband.

HE STILL LIVED in a boxcar, though one far fancier and more luxurious than the boxcar she'd lived in as a child. His caboose sported a narrow bed with flowered sheets and an orange-and-pink comforter, the kind of thing women from the church might have given him. He had kicked the bedding down to the foot of the bed, as if he'd had a restless night. The mattress itself had the old covered buttons and blue-and-white-striped ticking that she remembered from Italian sleeping cars, a luxury for the nuns going to Rome for their first and only visit. Pope John XXIII had paid for the order to send a delegation of nuns working directly with the poor, and Salina recalled the rocking motion that had lulled her to sleep and the marvel of a tangerine sun, rising above the Holy City.

Her father's worn overalls hung from a hook. She would take back to town. Surely the church had a clothes bin for the needy, though who could be needier than her father, she couldn't imagine. She would have to pick up some Woolite to wash his red flannel shirt; even a thrift shop wouldn't take dirty clothes. Across from the flannel shirt hung an undershirt whose underarms were the color of his windburnt face. In the small, silver-less mirror hanging from a nail, she imagined him pulling aside the skin of his jaw to approve the face he showed to the world, for, though a short man, he had always been vain about his high cheekbones and the skin of a man twenty years younger. Did her sister or brother have a photograph? Probably not.

AT THE FRONT of the caboose she found the kitchen and a garbage bag half full of empty cans. Her order hadn't allowed her to send him money. All her earnings went to a common fund. But whenever an employer or family member slipped her a twenty for some extra service — a fault of her compulsive tidying — she folded shirt-cardboard around the cash and sent it by mail to General Delivery, not even wanting the trail of a check because he'd never had a bank account and could only sign his name with his mark, a scribble that looked more like a cattle brand than an H.

A single hot plate was connected by a cracked pink hose to a propane canister on the floor. This could very well be the same burner her mother had used to feed a family of six. Or, maybe it was a hot plate he'd found discarded in an alley. Who knew? It did the job.

Always looking for scraps of corrugated roofing, discarded boards, or half-used cans of paint, he spent Sundays after Mass exploring. His walks took him through the alleys behind La Junta's neat grid of bungalows, the houses where Anglos lived. And if it wasn't shameful enough that their only shelter was a boxcar, where everyone in town knew the Limone family lived, over the years a subdivision of outhouse-sized buildings grew up around it. Her father decorated each little structure with hub caps and parts of bumpers. Each dwelling had a small door and a window with a single pane of glass. Hers was painted barn red, her sister's the yellow of egg yolk. Salina had been pleased to busy herself wiping the window and sweeping the floor, making believe it was a real house and hers alone. "If you want to be building these places for the children," Salina's mother had told him, "you should look for a third job." Hurt, he'd hopped down out of the boxcar, out of the chaos of toddlers and Salina's end-less rounds of blanket folding, sweeping, and changing the di-visions of the fruit crates that made up the low, splintered walls of the children's half. Off he'd go to drag more treasures home.

When she was young, the family's drinking water had come from an aluminum watering can of the kind farmers' wives used for their gardens. It sat by the boxcar's door, along with an alu-minum cup. Here in this caboose, she saw, he had upgraded to a much nicer water container, a two-gallon Coleman camping thermos. She pushed a button to see if the water had frozen. It had not.

Of the items stacked in a pyramid on a shelf, she saw cans of peaches, apricots, *menudo*, and one of Hormel tamales. On the counter sat a white enamel washbowl with a red rim, and in it, a plate with a dried brown crust and a dirty spoon, almost as if he had left it for her to wash up. The loaf of Wonder Bread in the bread box had not yet hardened. Squeezing it, she suddenly felt the freshness of his death.

Grieving could wait. Her stomach growled, and she wanted to get back for the dinner the deacon had promised. It wouldn't be right to leave without finding some way to be of service. After a drink of water, she gathered the cans and carried them to her father's room. Heat from the stove had warmed the caboose. She took a deep breath to inhale whatever remnant of his essence remained. All old men had their odors. She likened it to cloves or chewing tobacco, and as she made her hobo's bundle, she sniffed the objects that had been close to him. The only smell that called up a memory was a sliver of soap next to his razor. Fels-Naptha, a combination of mothballs and bay leaves, a smell she associated with her mother and the round steel tub in which she could clearly see her mother's hands working a shirt up and down on the corrugated washboard. No one used that soap nowadays. Fels-Naptha was for serious dirt — oil and black grease, or for the dirt embedded in the knees of overalls.

Turning, she looked over her shoulder at his mattress. Lifting it all the way up, she saw his hidey-hole, a single nail securing a coffee tin's ragged lid. She spun it sideways. Reaching into the hole, she felt around, her fingers touching something furry and stiff. She recoiled, and after catching her breath and telling herself not to be squeamish — she wiped people's asses for a living and if she could deal with excrement, this was nothing — she put her hand in the hole again.

Shredded paper. She pulled it all out, along with a poor dead mouse. The paper made up a punctured sheet that reminded her of the snowflakes from her long-ago days in school. Carefully she smoothed the paper across the mattress.

An official document of some kind. State of California. The name of a man she'd heard her father mention. Oliveira. At the bottom of the letter, she saw the man's brown-inked signature. How exactly this Oliveira had cheated her father, she could no longer remember, only that it had to do with why her father had fled California. He'd always told her there was money due, that he had papers to prove it, and she wondered if these had been the papers, the record of his years as a *bracero*. Maybe he'd kept them to show he'd existed, that the State of California had blessed the labor of his hands with its official, brown-bear seal.

She opened a latch on the wall below the bed to discover a storage space, empty apart from a train lantern whose chimney had not been washed and whose kerosene had hardened into a yellow bolus. Putting the lantern aside, she felt up where the papers had been and discovered the sharp corners of a wooden box. A cigar box. Tugging it, she tried to take it down, but her father had attached it so firmly it wouldn't budge.

FOURTH GRADE WAS the year they began living in La Junta. He had found the boxcar when he'd ridden into town from the ranch, and he had come all the way to Cheraw, where her mother had found a job changing sheets in a hotel, earning enough money to pay for the small adobe building out behind someone's modest brick home. And Salina remembered the cold ride in the back of a pickup truck, her mother holding her belly, and she, with her arms around her little sisters, shrunk down to keep the wind from tangling her hair. By the time they reached town it had been hours since they'd had a drink of water. Her mother had looked around the dusty streets and begun crying. "It will be fine," her father had promised. "Don't worry. I have prepared a new home, and it will cost us nothing to live there." It was a year after they'd settled in that the accident happened.

She remembered only that they hauled water from a red

pump at a farmhouse that had burnt down, and since she was the oldest, she walked with him to carry it home. Before the days of plastic, the containers — jerricans — weighed nearly as much as the liquid they held. She must have been nine or ten, maybe as old as eleven. It was when she still wanted to be with her father, when she desperately wanted to win his smile.

On this particular day, her father sang songs from his youth. It hadn't started snowing, or at least no snow had accumulated on the ground. Droplets of breath froze in her nostrils, and when she asked her father if he could pump the handle while she took a drink, he said yes, and told her to open her mouth.

She'd never been sure how her tongue attached itself to the handle. Maybe he'd told her to put it there. One of his odd little jokes. For a long time she'd thought so and held it against him, hated him even, but now she thought she'd made that up, one insult that stood for poverty's many insults. More likely some boy at school had put her up to it because it was a kid's prank. She only remembers that her father had shouted, "Don't do that!" and pushed her away, leaving her taste buds and a layer of skin. Youch!

The first month her tongue had bled and bled. Pulling off the gauze only made it bleed more, and she sat mute in the back row at school, not daring to speak. Even these many years later, there were still things she couldn't taste. Salt, for instance. Lemons. Parmesan cheese, which she could feel as gritty slivers, but never craved.

WHEN HE'D POINTED down the road at the caboose, the deacon had said he'd swing back by the church in an hour. She shut off the propane — no sense wasting fuel. The caboose turned instantly frigid. As she walked back, her burden of clothing grew heavier with each step.

Back at the church, she dropped the clothes by the ward-robe. She would ask Dr. Clancy if there was a woman with chil-dren who might like to cut up the fabric for a rag rug. That was what her mother would have done, cut every bit of fabric into inch-wide strips and sewn them end to end. A lifetime's work went into her mother's rug, which grew wider by the year, and eventually allowed them to step on the boxcar's floor with bare feet. Salina's job was to wind the endless rag-ball, and when she'd finished her homework, her eyes straining in the flicker-ing light of the kerosene lamp, she would pick up the wooden crochet hook and, sitting cross-legged on the floor, hook the rug's circumference, her hands always busy with that work or some other. Half asleep, she would have heard the boxcar's door slide its final inches shut or the poof as her father blew out the light and murmured in Spanish, "Sleep well, children."

There was so much to remember. The dry air. The way it opened her nostrils. The intermittent shush of passing cars. Dr. Clancy had left the nave's door ajar, and until he returned, she would give herself a moment of quiet reflection.

She pushed the door open, and there her father sat, hands on his knees, dressed in a black, wool suit with wide lapels, white hair slicked back in a ponytail. Hugo Limone. His skin no longer looked young. It had more wrinkles than any old man's she had ever seen, but if that skin had been plumped out by nourishment, hydration, and youth, she would have instantly recognized the man whose blessing she had not asked for when she left.

She remained standing by the altar, afraid that he was a ghost rather than the man who had sent a piece of his heart traveling with her wherever she went. Finally, the pounding in her chest subsided.

He stood and moved out of the pew. He had shrunk since she'd seen him last, or else she had grown.

Callused fingers pressed her cheeks. The skin of his finger-tips felt silky and cool. In the black irises of his eyes flashed tiny, moonlit windows. "*M'hijita.*" My little daughter.

A cry of rage and anguish escaped. Then she fell against his shoulder and allowed herself to be comforted.

TITO'S DESCENT

———o———

IF YOU LOSE a friend in his youth, the years after such a loss become a kind of afterlife, an unreality, as if you, yourself, are fixed in that time when death lies far in the future. At first, you miss them, and all the questions of whether there is a heaven immediately stand in your path. The person you love like a brother is gone, shimmering in the stream of memory, and that is the picture you carry forward, taking it out now and then and pondering how the miraculous and tragic can coexist.

Back in April 1968 when Tito led us down into the cavern, we had no fear of death nor suspicion that what we were about to find would splash our names across the Spanish newspapers, and indeed, the newspapers of the world. With the promise of a few *pesetas*, two local boys — mascots, of sorts — agreed to guide us. The boys said that our destination, a pothole called the Well of Ramu, had no bottom and that their grandmothers claimed it was haunted by evil spirits. The Well of Ramu was located atop a massive, limestone bluff. Shepherds, standing near it and looking out toward the Atlantic, had many a time been startled by the eerie-sounding moans of disembodied suffering.

Perhaps I should explain for the benefit of those urban dwellers who will watch your documentary that this "pothole" was not the kind of pothole one finds in cities, where the asphalt washes away and a street crew must be summoned to throw in a couple of shovelfuls of macadam. This was a geological pothole, a hole in the tabletop of a bluff into which a stray sheep or goat might fall to its death.

Neither Jesús nor Aurelio believed the old wive's tales, but they thought it well to warn us. They wanted to show us a different cave. Some crawling, but big grottoes and excellent formations. Most certainly worth the effort and "much easier for the girls," Jesús said from beneath the first traces of a mustache.

"Don't worry about the girls," Tito said, championing the three of us. "We go all together, or not at all."

Tito sprang over the stone fence that encircled the pothole and dropped to his knees. "The main thing is to determine how much rope we need."

Then, flattening himself on the ground and with a handful of rocks, he slid his shoulders over the abyss.

Potholes were new to our caving group. In fact, I had never heard of a pothole until Tito proposed this expedition. The guides were country boys and had never rappelled down into one either. Aurelio, the older of the two, warned us not to get too close to the edge in case our weight made the ground collapse; but curiosity got the better of them, and they, too, flattened themselves around the perimeter, cocking their ears and listening to see how long it took for Tito's stones to hit bottom.

Your cameraman asks why we spelunkers didn't lower a lantern. A lantern only works if the floor of the cave is near the surface. Otherwise, darkness swallows the light. We could only determine the depth by feel, so when Tito couldn't hear the stones strike bottom, he lowered a lead fishing weight, the hefty kind fishermen in Ribadesella once used to sink their nets in the ocean. I suppose they must still use them, come to think of it. As to where he'd found one, I don't recall precisely, but Tito was very careful about bringing whatever we might need for the caves he wanted to explore, and I think he must have borrowed the weight from a cousin. By the time we were finished with our preparations, we had five climbing ropes of eighty meters each tied together.

The plan, Tito said, gathering us around, was for him to descend first, assess the situation, and then send down one of the guides.

Instead of saying "of course," the guides looked at one another.

Aurelio, maybe fourteen, said that when the boys explored caves, they slithered along with flashlights until the batteries dimmed, at which point they backed out.

"Do you want to go down or not?" Tito said.

"I'm scared," Jesús, about thirteen, said, "but, yes. I'll try."

"One of you must stay behind."

"Can't we both go?" Aurelio said.

"It's better to draw straws," Tito said. "If we get injured down there, the one up here can run for help."

"Where should we go?" Aurelio said.

"The mayor's house," Tito said, nodding his head in the direction of the town across the river. "Or the Guardia Civil. And, if the one who draws the longest straw is still scared to jump into a dark hole, one of the women can show you how it's done."

The boys smirked at us girls.

The younger, Jesús, drew the short straw. "So, am I just supposed to wait here, or what?"

"Yes, wait," Tito said. "Once we're down, you're the only way we can communicate with the outside world."

Tito secured the rope around a boulder and attached carabiners to his climbing harness. Saluting, he slid over the lip.

Adolfo, a bull whose callused hands came from years of scything his father's hay, stood over the coil, the rope running around his leather-vested back and through his hands. Coun-terbalancing Tito's weight, he lowered our leader down.

THERE WERE TWELVE of us in the Torreblanca Speleological Society, mainly geology students at the university in Oviedo, plus Tito's sister and one of her friends. The name "Torreblanca" came from the town where Tito grew up. I know "Speleological Society" makes it sound like we were some kind of learned group, sitting around and drinking port and dis-cussing academic articles about rock strata, but we weren't a "society" at all. Our youngest was fifteen and the oldest twen-ty-two. Eight were geology students — always out in the field, gathering rocks and carrying them back to the lab to hammer apart and examine. Tito, though still not finished with his bac-calaureate, had already discovered his life's passion. Tito was a real rockhound, completely mad for rocks.

In order to join the Torreblanca Speleological Society, as founder and self-appointed president, Tito insisted that we each buy the basics: a helmet, carbon lamp, and Levi's from the store where workmen bought their clothes. For caving, he preferred rubber waders, but he let two of us get away with hik-ing boots — what he wore when he went out with his moun-taineering friends. His kit of chocks, carabiners, and climbing ropes filled the trunk of his car.

These days, when I think of Tito, I see him in that famous photograph: in his helmet and muddy, as we all were. Chin down, he is spooning cold beans from a can. We are all smiling and looking at him in wonder. His appetite had become a joke. Bony shoulders with a hunch that hinted at his shyness, all el-bows and skinny legs, Tito was a study in angularity. A shock of hair hung over his forehead, and the camera caught him look-ing down into the can. If I have one regret, it is that Fernando, our unofficial Society photographer, having lined us up, did not say, "Tito, *amigo*, look at the camera." I should so have liked to see the tiny windows of light in Tito's coal-black eyes.

WE LATER LEARNED that the Well of Ramu was actually four hundred meters deep, the length of four football fields, and because of its depth, the temperature remained a constant ten degrees Celsius, barely above freezing. The caves we had explored before this were not quite as cold and often high up, generally an opening on the face of a cliff. To reach them we had to climb, and afterwards, rappel down the rock face. To do that, we slid the rope under our behinds and then leaned back, letting the rope play out as we backed down or bounced down the vertical wall. In the case of the Well of Ramu, we had no wall with which to brace our feet. When we dropped into the pothole, the rope slid through our gloveless hands.

I was supposed to show Aurelio how to manage the rope, but as I lowered myself down, I found that even twining my legs around it barely slowed my fall. By the time I reached bottom, my hands burned, and blisters were already forming. I pressed my palms together, wishing the pain would stop, and took a step back from the rope, my waders sinking in. Mud over-topped them.

"Watch out!" I cried. "Quicksand!"

Tito had been standing nearby and grabbed my arm. "I think we've landed in a riverbed."

"It's the San Miguel," said Aurelio, letting go of the rope and dropping freely the last three meters.

And, indeed, the sound of water echoed through the chamber, a gurgle that made me think we might step into the channel and be washed downstream. The things I feared most in caves were being sucked by the force of a river that would be too powerful to resist or stepping out into space and dropping into a lower chamber. My armpits began to tingle and, despite the cold, sweat formed on my upper lip.

Partly to overcome this aversion to confined spaces and partly because of Tito himself, I had joined his club, and now that he had accepted me, I dared not confess that in narrow passages, where I had neither room to turn around nor squirm and where I could see only the boots of the person crawling ahead, I feared the rock would shift and crush me.

The two other girls followed next, and then studious Fernando, who had a crush on Tito's sister, but was too shy to ask her out. Adolfo, whom Tito called "the human crane," came next, and finally little Ruperto, the youngest member, age fifteen. A lighter snapped briefly, illuminating his profile, and a moment later, I made out the glowing tip of his cigarette. Trying to appear older, no doubt.

We had all made it down safely.

"Let's see where we are," Tito said. "Each of you turn a hundred and eighty degrees and take five steps."

We did and, in the faint illumination of our carbide lamps, saw that the mud, the murky grayish-brown of a tidal flat, extended beyond the reach of our beams. The cave smelled like no other cave we'd been in before, the air dank and humid, like an ice box exploding with rotting cheese and moldy bread. The river, hidden from view, sounded close, but to reach it and possibly follow it to where it emerged from the earth, we would have to cross the reeking, gray pudding of mud.

The pothole, through which we had descended, and the rope, our only way out, stood behind us, and I was tempted to turn around and keep a hand on it. Were it not for the light falling from above, I could not have told up from down. It was discombobulating.

"Now take five more steps," Tito said, as if we were playing "Mother, May I?"

When the group had spread out so that each person, leaving his companions, felt a chilling awareness of the cold, Tito said to stand completely still and tilt back our heads.

I did.

Looking up, I could not see the top of the cavern, only a barricade of stalactites as evenly spaced as the twisted, iron bars on a window.

"Which way, do you think?" Tito asked the guide.

"To the right," Aurelio said, sounding assured for his age.

"To the right it is," Tito said.

And, then, as if needing to justify himself further, the guide said, "The air is cooler in that direction, and the sound of the river louder. This way should take us to the cave I told you of."

"And?" Tito said.

"From there we should be able to walk out."

"But you don't know that for certain?"

"I don't know if the passage is open," Aurelio said.

"Let's take a quick look," Tito said.

"What about us?" I asked on behalf of the female contingent.

"All for one, and one for all." Tito waved his hand inclusively, beckoning us to follow.

His and Aurelio's lamps bobbed toward the burbling water, its sound magnified by the echo chamber of the cave. A drop of water landed on my cheek, but when I looked up, I still could see no more than I would have seen in my grandmother's windowless root cellar.

Walking away from the rope had plunged me into darkness. As I rocked forward, mud sucked the wader from my heel. I tested each step and waited for the ground to render itself firm. The others cried out and cursed the sucking mud. It was impossible to move quickly, and I was breathing hard by the time I could see that rocks and boulders blocked our way. I placed my hand on one of the boulders and stopped. Had the stone dislodged from the ceiling, or had the river carried it in? Maybe Tito could tell. Meanwhile, the hiss of carbide, snaking up the tube on my back, reminded me of the hissing, slithering, eyeless albino salamanders we had seen in another cave. I hoped we wouldn't come upon any creatures like that in this airless space.

So far I hadn't felt the air movement Aurelio claimed would lead us to the other cave, and I began to think it would be better for us to stay in this large chamber where, at least, we could look back and see the shaft of light beaming down from the pothole. Tito told us to wait while they explored, and if this didn't prove to be a passageway, we could search the cavern for another.

Tito squeezed sideways through pointed, egg-shaped rocks as gigantic as those the Arabic astronomer Ibn Yunus was said to have used as gnomons. Meanwhile, Aurelio ducked into a fissure that looked as though it led to another cavern, and I thought he might find another big room, but without the river running through it. Shivering and hugging ourselves, we heard his boots splash through water and Tito cautioning Aurelio to watch his footing. When they found themselves in the same passageway, Tito called back and said they could stand upright, but not see daylight. That meant the walk out could take a long time.

At last, their lamps bobbed back in our direction.

They had been gone half an hour, and I had no confidence that we could get out this way. What if we encountered more blockages? It might be better to follow the river in the other direction. I turned toward the sound of water. Above me, I saw a flash of red. It startled me.

"What's that?" I asked.

"What's what?" Tito said.

"Red."

"Where?"

Looking up and trying to relocate the color on an over-hanging rock, I moved sideways from the boulder. Because I had taken my attention momentarily from the ground, my feet slipped, and I fell, scraping my blistered hands.

"This is so screwed!" I said. "It's black as midnight."

Then Tito had me by the elbow. His lamp blinded me, and my heart thrummed in my ears. Unlike the others, I was an art student, and the vividness of that red could only mean one thing: paint. I squinted, looking in vain as my headlamp's faint beam moved across the undulating rock above my head.

And then I saw it: the charcoal silhouette. A single horse's head. The horse had ears, nostrils, and the same throat latch — that thickening on the bottom of its muzzle — as hors-es in the pastures of Ribadesella. What was different was its mane. The mane stood as stiff as a zebra's.

"Look up there." I pointed.

"It's a horse," Tito whispered. He put his arm around me and drew me closer. He was trembling.

I had never been as aware of my body as I was at that mo-ment. The warmth of another human being, the sideways pres-sure of his hip, the squeeze of his fingers against my arm, the ripple of sensation from my forehead to my feet, made me feel as if we humans were designed, on a primitive level, to connect with one another not just with words, but with the intimacy of touch; that touch was essential for our well-being and the reason we have bodies, not just souls.

The others joined us, and Tito released me. Once again our leader, he directed us to form a line and tilt our heads in uni-son. Tito's sister, Eloisa, squeezed between us and put her arm around me.

Hefty little Pilar, one of the most irreverent women I've ever met, had her arm around my hip. "What gives?"

"Cave paintings," I said.

"Like at Altamira?"

"Well, we're not far from there."

Our lamps illuminated a swath of red.

"Is that blood?" Pilar asked.

"No. Ocher or iron oxide."

Honestly, at the time, I had no idea what kind of pigment paleolithic artists might have used. I only surmised that blood would have darkened and chipped away.

The artist had applied an orange-red wash to the cave wall just below the horse's head. In the illumination of our combined head lamps, a herd of horses jumped from the darkness. Six that we could see immediately, although with better light, the archaeologists would later document more. The herd faced the opposite direction and appeared to move across a plain of red that might have been grasslands set afire.

Of these figures, the best preserved was a mare in the fullness of pregnancy. Horizontal bands of black and white circled her legs, reminding me of the leggings of mimes who perform in traveling circuses. The stripes gave the mare a comical aspect, and most remarkably, the artist had painted her body violet. Could it be that horses in prehistory were violet? In every other respect the horse was as realistic as if Goya himself had rendered the image.

We lingered, tracing the animals with our fingers and seeing if others agreed that, yes, that was a horse. Or perhaps a deer, for as we continued to examine the figures, we saw that some had antlers.

Our watches told us that the day had advanced past one o'clock, and though we had filled our metal canisters with carbide pellets, we had a maximum of four total hours before the fuel ran out.

We walked as a group around the cavern, unable to locate any other painted surface.

THE TORREBLANCA SPELEOLOGICAL Society was not a democracy, but Tito asked our preference. Should he attempt to monkey-climb the four hundred meters of rope and prepare to pull us out, or should we follow the river, in which case, we should get going or have Jesús send down more carbide just in case. Like coal miners, cavers have always used carbide lamps because the lamps can be refilled and the fuel costs next to nothing. With the river below, we would have water, and could add it to the canisters when the gas pellets fizzled out. The main thing was not to get stuck down here in the dark.

The group split evenly, six to six. We gathered around the rope and Tito called up to Jesús. Expecting to see his face looking down, I was stunned when he did not answer.

Tito turned abruptly toward Aurelio. "Did your friend run off?"

Aurelio nervously cupped his hands around his mouth and shouted.

Still no Jesús.

"Maybe he got bored," Aurelio said.

If the passage proved to be a dead end, we'd have to come back here and wait, but that would have posed its own problem. The ground was too muddy to sit.

"We need more carbide," I said.

"I'll get some." Tito extinguished his lamp and took off his helmet. "Back in a second."

Hand over hand, he ascended the rope, twisting it between his muddy galoshes. When he made it to the first knot, he rested and looked down.

"You can do it!" we shouted in unison. His face took on a look of determination. At the second knot he rested again, this time, calling up angrily, "Jesús, you lazy lout! Come over here."

Jesús did not appear.

Halfway up the third section of rope, Tito began to slide.

He tried to slow his descent at the second knot by clamping it between his insteps. That helped, but unlike when I had abseiled in, with the rope acting as a swing beneath my butt, Tito had no such control and landed beside us with a thud.

Determined to try again, he prepared to remove his galoshes.

"Let me try," Aurelio said.

Our young guide did not even make it past the first section. By now, mud had made the rope too slippery to hold.

Tito put his helmet back on, and Ruperto took out his lighter and lit another cigarette.

"So, it's to be the river," Tito said. "Aurelio, what is your opinion? Downstream or up?"

"My instinct tells me up."

"Mine, too," Tito said. "Back to the passageway."

The prospect of discovering more paintings made us avid to stay underground, but not having the use of the rope made escape a necessity. Before we tore ourselves away from these paintings and began our trek to the exit, Aurelio ducked back into the fissure he'd explored. There he found a small chamber with deer incised on rock. Not painted deer. These were petroglyphs and finding them made him glad to have won the coin toss. Now, he could legitimately say he was the discoverer of the cave, or at least part of it.

Expecting more discoveries, we picked our way along the rock-strewn passage, our feet slipping on the slimy stones and me fearing that we would reach a dead end or an underground channel that would force one of us to submerge and try to swim against the current.

"Tito," I called out, my voice swallowed in the dark. "What if our lamps go out?"

"I have some extra carbide," he said, "and a dozen candles, but I suggest we not think of that and sing to keep up our spirits."

"What shall we sing?" Maria Pia called.

"How about 'Puppet on a String'?" Tito suggested.

Adolfo and Fernando began whistling, and the melody carried us along; however, we were concentrating so hard on where to put our feet that the lyrics simply drifted away.

AFTER THREE KILOMETERS underground, we caught the scent of fresh air. Just as the first sign of daylight appeared, our lamps sputtered out.

Ordinarily, when a cave is discovered, it's a shepherd who stumbles in, usually unappreciative, which is why so few caves are recorded or mapped. But the Well of Ramu was different. No one knew it was there. We were the first.

Since then the cave has changed. Despite the three air locks, the new artificial tunnel introduces outside air, and the unforgettable smell is gone. No one can experience it as we did fifty years ago.

It annoys me that I must pay an admission fee to bring my grandchildren, and it annoys me when people complain about the path being uneven and rocky and dimly lit. The last time I went there, a French-speaking woman was complaining to the guide, who happened to be Aurelio's son, that she'd had to walk a long way back just to see a few paintings. She had expected more for her money.

When I heard this, I felt a tremendous sense of abandonment and loss. "You have been privileged to see one of the treasures of the world," I said, "and yet you disparage it. This is not the same experience as going to the cinema."

I wanted to tell her what a miracle it was to stand before those paintings for the first time, to wonder at the artists who painted them and held them sacred. To imagine the horses that must have been running wild. And I wanted to tell her about Tito, how vibrant and alive he had been as we probed these secret grottoes. How he dove into his can of cold beans right after we had made it back to the top of the bluff and startled Jesús, taking a *siesta*. How euphoric we were as we tore off our muddy clothes and had Aurelio direct us to the mayor's house.

WOULD YOU MIND turning off the camera? Good. Now I will answer your question. Do I think Tito was a risk taker? Certainly, no more than any other young man his age, an age that predisposes the male of the species to believe he will live forever. Tito had his full share of the invincibility hormone. It surged through his veins, and it was what drew us to him.

Tito was brave. A leader. He believed in living life to the fullest, squeezing every drop of joy possible from his time on earth. And, remember, this was 1968, seven years before Franco's death. In a certain way, to live boldly was an act of political defiance.

When Tito slipped in a mountaineering accident a few days later, his sister brought us the news. The Faculty in Oviedo called for a day of mourning. The train to Torreblanca filled with students, but we, who knew him best, drove. At the Mass, his father wept like a man who'd lost a part of his very soul. And because of Señor Bustillo's intense grief, the authorities decided to name the cave in Tito's honor. No longer the Well of Ramu, today it is the Cave of Tito Bustillo.

Just this morning, I was thinking about Tito, how he stood next to me in that cave and how my body rippled with pleasure. Tito and I might have had a future. Instead, what he gave me was a single moment of ecstasy. Following his example, I have sought to live every moment as if it were my last.

LONG TIME, NO SEE

———o———

J UDY MONAGHAN WAS Tom's stepmother, half of the
sack-race team of Jude and Gene that had hopped around
the Midwest, following their own good time, or whim. For all
the years of Tom's growing up, his dad had been absent, working at a meatpacking plant in Kansas City, following the oil
boom to Omaha, making book at Indiana Downs, and finally,
returning to Hammond after smoking had ruined his lungs.
And when that tired, shuffling old man had shown up on Tom's
doorstep, Tom had stood for a moment before opening the
screen door and telling him to come in.

Back then, Tom had something to prove, if only to himself.
He was a different kind of man than his father had been. He
was responsible. Trustworthy. A man his family could depend
on. Now his dad was dead, and Tom had allowed himself to
imagine that Judy, *aka* "Jude", his stepmother, would just float
up into the stratosphere like a helium balloon. Instead, she kept
after him to visit, so here he was, pushing open the revolving
door of Grace Place, preparing to watch the 1999 Super Bowl
on his dad's Toshiba.

The atrium was what his dad Gene had liked best about
living at Grace Place. The cost was one thing, but the company

another. Enjoying the sunlight that beamed down through the glass, half a dozen old men gathered around a console television turned up to maximum volume. Two women were knitting. A half-finished puzzle lay on the card table. Rubber plants potted in ceramic urns had dropped leaves on the terrazzo floor, and no one had bothered to sweep them up. The weekend employees found every possible excuse to avoid extra work. Lazy bastards. *However, not my problem*, Tom thought, heading for the elevator.

Quilted silver blankets protected the walls — protected the old people, too, from lurches and falls, not that the elevator moved at anything faster than a snail's pace. Except for the shitty elevator, what a good deal this subsidized retirement center had been: two meals a day, rock-bottom rent, a quarter of the nothing these old people had to live on. Years from now, when Tom would move into a one-bedroom on the third floor and haul an oxygen tank when he went down for meals, he would think back to Super Bowl XXXIII and the odd symmetries of life, how fate, or perhaps his own weak nature, had looped around and brought him back full circle to a time and place he had never expected to see again.

On six, the doors opened. His Navajo belt buckle was cutting into his flesh, and he stuck his fingers down his Levi's to adjust himself. Gene and Jude's studio stood at the far end of the balcony, the "penthouse suite" Jude called it. The taps on Tom's motorcycle boots clicked on the concrete floor, and as he rounded a corner, he saw her leaning against the half-wall that overlooked the atrium.

"Long time, no see, handsome." Jude seized his arms and pulled him close.

"Jesus, Jude." He levered her shoulders back. "Cutting off the circulation."

Her face crackled with good humor, this tiny woman Gene

129

had called "my little Roman candle" and who Tom's mom called "Judy Home-wrecker". Like a schoolgirl, Jude wore a brown, corduroy jumper with dollar-sized buttons. White bangs covered the tops of her tortoise-shell glasses, mended with tape. Fingerprints smudged the lenses.

"Don't you wash those things?" Tom said.

"I can see good enough." She grinned. "What's your favorite color?"

"Red, I guess."

"Your truck's red, isn't it?"

"Piece of shit, that thing."

"Well, take that piece of shit to the junkyard."

"What?"

She pushed him toward the apartment's door. "Let's go watch the game. You'll see."

"What am I supposed to see?"

"Turn on the TV. Oh, and excuse the mess. I haven't had time to run the vacuum."

On both sides of the entry hall hung pictures of Tom, his kids, and grandkids. He straightened the picture of Eileen. Still a Mass-goer, and not just on Easter and Christmas, Tom's sister Eileen was temporarily on the outs with Jude. Or, maybe, the other way around.

Tom noticed that the bed wasn't where it used to be. Jude had gotten someone to push it into a corner. On the wall above it hung the Mayor's honorary key that Tom had sand-cast from the City of Chicago mold—Gene's personal key to the city.

Now, four rust-colored bedspreads draped over what looked like piles of boxes. Between the mesas were canyons barely wide enough for a person to squeeze through. The carpet had vanished beneath a Grand Canyon of crap.

"Good grief," Tom said. His stepmother had become a fuckin' hoarder. *But, hey,* he thought. *Not my problem.* He had come for the Super Bowl. If Jude wanted to live in a pigsty, let her.

"Go ahead, sit." She encouraged him to take the recliner that had been his dad's.

"Where's your chair?" he said.

"I gave it away."

"Where are you going to sit?"

"I need to keep an eye out." Jude made her way around the piles, doing like his sister's retarded kid, patting her way, fingers spread. Gene would have had a stroke if he'd seen this. Hell, Gene did have a stroke.

The TV screen was dark. Tom had gone to Best Buy and then borrowed a moving dolly to get the big Toshiba up here. The flat-sceen, top-of-the-line for its day, had a Multi-Window, dual-tuner picture and a 28-watt sound system, and when he'd finally installed anchors for the swivel mount and set up the speakers, his dad, a laconic, ex-Navy man, had actually cracked a smile.

"I thought you'd be glued to the game," Tom said, looking around at the piles.

"You better turn it on," she said.

"Where's the remote?" Tom said.

"Somewheres."

"Don't you watch TV?"

"Not much."

Next time, if there was a next time, he'd bring his tools. No point leaving the TV if she wasn't going to watch it. He could put it in his mom's room. Pretend it was a present.

He pressed the power button. The fourth quarter had already begun. Jude must have diddled with the controls. The color was all messed up. Brent Mussburger looked greenish, like the fake antique frogs they cast at the foundry. All yesterday, Tom had been dipping the castings in a sulfur bath. He sniffed his fingers. Bad egg smell. His nails were black. He took out a pen knife and flipped open the blade. Mom would have a shit fit, seeing him drop nail jam on the rug, but Jude didn't care. At least he could relax here. His nephew Kenny, eleven, wasn't drooling or needing his diaper changed. His mom wasn't on his case about adding a grab bar to the shower. Perched on the arm of the recliner, he leaned forward and squeezed his fingers into the control panel's partly open door. Faces turned red.

Jude slapped the window. "We're up here! We're up here!" She cupped her eyes and pressed her nose to the glass.

Then Tom felt her arms go around his middle. The hold reminded him of his nephew Kenny, wanting a horsey-back ride. He twisted away. "Come on, Jude. Act your age."

He had a slight headache from the night before, celebrating Mom's birthday with a barbecue. She'd been living at his place a month, and to bug her, he'd had one too many beers. He felt a little top heavy and unsteady, like one of the foundry's brass floor lamps. He needed his base filled with sand for ballast, except, he'd settle for a screwdriver or Vodka Collins or even a shot of Scotch.

Jude edged past and went into the bathroom. Moments later, she cracked open the door. "Don't let them leave."

"Let who leave?"

"You'll see."

He lifted the corner on one of the orange bedspreads. Boxes underneath. How nuts this would have made Gene, seeing the place like this. But, hey, Jude was a big girl. He heard the whist of hair spray and put a bandanna over his nose. Working at the foundry, he'd managed to wreck his lungs. He was always coughing stuff up. Today, he'd put that out of his mind, too.

Anyhow, the Broncos had a solid 17-3 lead over the Falcons. If the Bears had a quarterback like Elway, they'd have a chance. What an arm! And he was retiring this year. Lucky duck.

Tom still had ten to go, if he made it that far. The company had started outsourcing to Malaysia.

"I'm ready!" Jude opened the bathroom door. Her eyes sparkled like the MagicKist billboard on I-94.

"You have a date, or what?" he said.

She pointed to the ceiling. "Gene's bringing us good luck."

"Jude, what's going on here?"

She pointed at the window. "Take a look for yourself."

Not really seeing the point, Tom eased himself from the recliner and went to the window. Grime from Hammond's now defunct factories—metallic, sooty, abrasive—etched the glass. In the turnaround, the driver of an Ambulette was folding up a hydraulic lift. A male attendant in a white uniform, one of the home-health aides they let you hire for a maximum of three weeks, pushed a woman in a wheelchair toward the front door.

"Am I supposed to know her?" Tom said.

"How do I look?" Jude held out her skirt. "They say you look heavier on TV. Or is it lighter?"

Tom turned slowly back to the woman being wheeled toward the door. He hoped the broken bone, or whatever it was, would heal fast. Grace Place did monthly assessments. If you weren't well enough to live independently, you were up and out, and all the convalescent homes that took Medicaid assignment strapped patients in chairs. Gene's life had ended in a nursing home like that. During a year and a half of Sunday visits and with Gene, hollow-cheeked and looking like someone whose mind had been shop-vacced out, Tom had seen what lay ahead. Problem was, you couldn't take care of yourself—lay off the booze, join the Y—and take care of a million other people, too. In all that set of women who depended on him, Tom was the only wage earner, Eileen's bum-of-a-husband having bailed.

The game ended, but Tom hardly noticed. He and Jude needed to talk. Looked like things were a little out of control.

"Why don't I run down to the 7-Eleven for some cheese and crackers?" he asked.

"You can't do that. This is the exciting part."

"The post-game show?"

Jude looked toward the door, then plunked herself in the recliner. She leaned forward, hands on knees. On the screen, a white van pulled into the driveway of a suburban house. Two men and a woman carrying Mylar balloons knocked on a door. A man in glasses and a yellow sweater opened it. The visitors thrust the balloon-strings into his hand.

Jude sprang up. "No!" She hurried from the apartment and, standing on tiptoe at the wall, shouted down into the atrium. "Why didn't you tell them to come up here? I was waiting." She was nearly hysterical and on the verge of tears.

Coming up behind Jude, Tom let his hand rest on her shoulder. Down below, the circle of game-watching men were intent on the highlights. Looked like they didn't even hear her.

Jude settled back on her heels. "You don't have to worry, Tommy. I'm not going to jump."

"That never even occurred to me."

He took her arm and guided her safely back inside. It wouldn't be a bad idea for the management to put up some kind of guard rail on the balconies. He'd make a note and drop it in the suggestion box.

"The Prize Patrol couldn't find us, Tommy," she said.

"The Prize Patrol wasn't looking. They didn't come here."

"But the white van — "

"You think they're gonna send the Prize Patrol in an Ambulette?"

"Ambulette, my ass! It was my van, the one they promised me."

In the apartment he made her sit, then threw back a bedspread. A brown, fur stole covered a stack of books, all of them still in their cardboard sleeves. *Herbal Healing. The ABC's of Computers. Fun & Games for Kids.* A Styrofoam take-out container sat on a folded American flag, probably the one from Gene's coffin.

"Christ Almighty!" Tom brandished the container. "Don't you throw anything away?"

"I start, and then I can't decide."

He found the kitchen trash. Then he leaned for a moment on the counter and let his head drop against the cupboard. When he returned, she was still sitting where he'd left her.

"Jude, how long has this been going on?" he said.

Muttering, she pawed through cigar boxes of loose bullets, lucky pennies wrapped in paper and marked with the dates they were found, and envelopes slit with a letter opener. "I called in to this psychic on TV, and she said it was my lucky year."

Watching her, Tom felt alternately hot and tight, like a piece of metal being bent back and forth until fatigue sets in and it snaps.

An obstinate, head-held-high Jude handed him an envelope. "Read this. It says here I made it to the final round. They wanted directions to my house. I wrote them back. Maybe I gave them a bum steer. Your dad said I never could navigate. Or maybe it was the elevator. Everyone says its poky."

Tom unfolded a letter. "Dear Judith Monaghan: You have been a loyal customer. You are among the select few in our final round."

He put on his reading glasses and examined the fine print. "Jude, says here you only have one in a hundred-fifty-million chance of winning. That's half the population of the United States! This is a letter they send out to everyone."

She frowned. "But they said I'm loyal, Tommy."

"Loyal. Okay, I'll give you that."

"Why would they say such a thing?"

"To keep you hooked."

"Tommy, I wanted the money for you." Now she sounded just plain disappointed.

"Money's not that big a deal," he said.

"For Kenny, then."

"Kenny."

"Eileen's little boy."

"He's big now."

"But he still needs clothes, don't he? Like you needed clothes after your daddy left, and your momma didn't have a pot to piss in. Oh, Tommy, I feel so bad. They came, and when they couldn't find us, they went somewheres else." Her voice trailed off.

"Everything there is to know about you is in some computer's brain," Tom said. "Besides, people like us, we never win."

"I know what I know."

"Jude." He held her chin. "Look at me. It's a scam."

She took back the letter and folded it in thirds.

"Go ahead. Keep it," he said.

"Really?" Her glasses slid down to the tip of her nose.

Tom plucked them off. "Let me wash those things."

In the galley kitchen, he squirted dish soap on the lenses. The Scotch tape holding the temple fell off. The screw had dropped out, maybe not the only loose screw as far as Jude was concerned.

He changed the channel to a nature show and made her sit. On the big screen, a doe grazed in shrubs that winter had stripped bare. The doe's eyes, dumb and fearful, were the eyes he had been trying not to see behind Jude's glasses.

In a junk drawer he found a yellowed roll of Scotch tape and a safety pin. Before he gave back her mended glasses, they had to talk.

He lowered the footrest of the recliner and knelt beside her.

"So, tell me what's going on, Jude."

She covered her face and rocked back and forth, like Kenny, banging his head against the wall. "I'm in Dutch, kid."

"Been cheating at bingo?"

"Tommy, they're going to kick me out."

"I expect."

He looked at the envelopes and jewelry boxes and the coffee-table books about places Jude would never go. All of it would have to be gone through. The weather was too damn cold, or he would have hopped on his Harley and taken off for Indiana Dunes.

Jude reminded him of his sister Eileen, a good girl and a good soul, who listened with that same attentive and dumb-struck stare whenever Father McNally or the President or any male in a position of authority told her what to do. Beneath the shoeboxes on the desk, Tom saw Gene's black-and-white Navy snapshots under thick, greenish glass. She lived by the rules of another era. Now Jude had dementia. She wasn't equipped.

"Do you know where I could find some garbage bags?" he said.

"I should know, shouldn't I."

He gave back her glasses, and she put them on.

"These are much better, Tommy. You're so good to me."

"Not really," he said. "Not really at all."

But he would do better.

VOICES

———◦———

A YEAR AFTER she had buried her husband, Neva Roth sat in a Viennese rehearsal hall listening to the piece she had dedicated to his memory. A mixed chorus of men and women, packed tight on risers erected in a semi-circle behind the orchestra, sang a modern version of a Gregorian plainsong chant. The choir could handle her kind of avant-garde music. They sang Schoenberg, for heaven's sake. But in the orchestra, the percussion section sounded like waiters dropping trays of crockery. A bassoon belched out low groans. Piccolos scratched glass. There was no unity and no beauty, and it was because of the conductor, carving mountains with his baton. She put down her copy of the score.

"Hold on a minute," she said.

Herr Lautner, wings of wild hair above his ears, glanced back. "Yes?"

Neva approached the podium, expecting to be given a hand up. Tall and elegant at seventy-four, she had paid her dues and was rightfully entitled to every courtesy.

"Sit down, Frau Roth!" Lautner said.

"You're not interpreting the score correctly." She turned to the orchestra and made a fist. "I want from the heart." Then to Lautner, *sotto voce*, she said, "They're playing mechanically. Why don't you try directing without the baton?" Hands up like a ballerina, she traced a heart in the air.

"Madam, in all my years of conducting, I have never had a composer tell me how to do my job."

"But you seemed stuck in the middle," Neva said.

"I am not *stuck*, Madam. This is my method."

"But spontaneity—"

"Please, Madam! Enough!" His baton clattered to the floor.

No one took a breath, not the musicians, waiting tensely to go on, nor the chorus. As a gesture of conciliation, she picked up the baton and handed it to him.

He tapped the podium and raised his arms. Sweat darkened his armpits. The rehearsal space was not air conditioned. What's wrong with you, Neva, she thought, settling back into her front row seat. Give him the benefit of the doubt. Some conductors preferred to work alone. Indeed, she was one of them. Maybe he'd been forced to invite her to rehearsal.

At seventy-two, she was well-known in New York, but a stranger here. Tomorrow was the debut of "Falling in Flight," a tone poem based on the legend of Icarus. Happy Icarus, soaring on his wax wings toward the sun, and terrified Icarus when the wings melted. She desperately needed Lautner to get onboard.

BUT ONBOARD HOW? Should she talk to him? Try sending an email? She thought she had given him enough guidance before rehearsals began. However, maybe it wasn't him at all. There was a good possibility that the piece itself was flawed.

For months she had tried to create new work, but Martin's death had disrupted the twilight sleep from which her music sprang. She was having trouble contacting her heart, the breath and flesh and voice that went into her compositions withered by that last glimpse of Martin's face, powdered and peach-colored. Something within her had shriveled—her daring, her boldness, her belief that in the face of life's great events, music mattered. But, of course, it mattered. Otherwise, why had she decided not to have children? Why else had she thought the sacrifice worth it?

Wrung out by the humidity, Lautner's refusal to accept an apology and the *u-bahn's* rush hour crowds, she rode the escalator up to street level. A bad rehearsal would not matter if the concert went well. She wanted the piece played exactly as she heard it in her head.

PENSION ACLON ON tiny Dorotheergasse occupied the top floor of an old apartment building. From the foyer, a marble staircase spiraled up and around the open shaft of a bird-cage elevator. Neva's euro in the coin box brought the motor to life. She got in, punched the button for her floor, and the elevator glided up, pulleys shrieking, to the sixth level, where it jerked to a halt inches below the landing. Almost home, and none too soon.

The concierge, a heavyset, middle-aged woman with features elongated by a severe bun, greeted her in the hall. "A Herr Hoffmann left a number for you to call."

"I don't know anyone by that name." Neva took the hastily scribbled message, crumpled it, and stuffed it in her pocket. Probably some flunky of the conductor's.

In a room where lace curtains covered the open windows, she unpacked her suitcase into the walnut *schrank* and thought how proud she'd been to receive the commission. Martin's family came from Vienna, and she'd been dying to see it for years. Now Lautner was putting his autocratic stamp on her work. But what could she do? Nothing.

On the far side of the bed, she spread out Martin's red nightshirt, arms akimbo. The nightshirt had the well-loved appearance of Martin himself, bear-like in girth. Forget dinner. She threw back the duvet and kicked off her heels. If she could just get some sleep.

The phone jangled. The concierge. A Herr Hoffmann awaited her in the breakfast room. Neva slammed down the receiver. The conductor refused to speak with her in person, and now sent his minion to tell her what? That her work was atonal? Too difficult to play?

Down the hall, a crystal chandelier hung above eight round tables set with crisp white linen and gold-rimmed china, but the room was only used in the morning, and the man who sat reading the pages of the *Wiener Tagblatt* sat in virtual darkness, the paper held high to capture what little light came from the alley windows. He was impeccably dressed in a khaki suit; his long legs were crossed at the knee, and one thin-soled Italian loafer bobbed evenly, as if he were keeping time to a slow internal metronome.

"You woke me," she said, rather coldly.

The man folded his paper, slipped his reading glasses into a breast pocket, and stood in one smooth motion. Before she could withdraw her hand, he pressed it to his lips. When he straightened, she saw that his face was tan and weather-cracked, his eyes merry. He was quite handsome. Pleased, but puzzled, she regarded him.

"*Gnädige Frau.* I see you do not have the slightest idea who I am."

"Should I?"

"We met in Salzburg," he said, his voice a pleasing tenor.

"Didn't the conductor send you here?"

"No, no. We met in a beer garden."

Ah, yes. Now she remembered. Half a dozen Austrians, all her age or a little older, had taken seats at a nearby outdoor table, and over beer and pretzels she had told them about her commission.

"Were you one of the music *aficionados* from Vienna?"

"Exactly," he said, pulling out the chair to his side and gesturing for her to sit. "When I saw the poster advertising the Schoenberg concert, I remembered you."

"Oh, the concert!" she groaned, sinking into the seat. "I committed a *faux pas* and practically got myself booted out of rehearsal."

"Do you not remember me inviting you to accept my hospitality in Vienna?"

"In America that kind of comment is never sincere."

"No? But many Americans say to look them up if I ever return to the States."

"You'd better not." Neva laughed, the first time in ages. "They'd be surprised."

"But I am Austrian and meant it." He smiled broadly and handed her a business card.

She ran her thumb across the raised engraving. With her rusty High German, she translated the words. "'Offices, renovations, restorations.' What are you, an architect?"

"Architect and urban planner." He saluted. "With a degree from NYU."

"How did you find me?"

"A friend in the choir told me where you were staying, so I tracked you down."

"Well, then."

"The concert is sold out," he said. "Sometimes a loose ticket is floating about in the director's pocket. Perhaps you could ask?"

"I wouldn't dare," she said.

"I apologize," he said. "At this late date, you and Herr Lautner must have VIPs to think about."

"Herr Lautner doesn't confide in me."

"Oh? A bit of trouble with the Maestro?"

"He doesn't seem to have a feel for the piece. It's torture watching him rehearse."

"Herr Lautner has a reputation for being... shall we say, overly methodical."

"I'm actually relieved to know that. I thought he was either clueless or trying to purposefully sabotage the performance. Today's rehearsal wiped me out."

"Then I'm sorry for bothering you with my ticket problems. You must want to rest." He folded the newspaper under his arm. "I'll get out of your hair."

"Wait," she said. "I have an extra ticket." The one they had sent for Martin. She hurried to her room and got it. When she returned, he was waiting in the hall.

"Then you must allow me to reciprocate and show you Vienna. Are you free the day after tomorrow?"

"Yes, certainly, Herr Hoffmann, and I'd be grateful for the diversion."

"Please call me Otto."

His move toward familiarity caught her off guard.

"All right — Otto."

There was a post-concert reception. Realizing it might be awkward to abandon him, she invited him to come, and he accepted.

NEVA SLEPT THROUGH the morning rehearsal. Not jet lag. She wished it were. Even in New York she often overslept, made early appointments and then forgot to set an alarm. She called the choir's secretary and lied about a migraine. Seeing Otto's card on the nightstand, she dialed his number.

"Did we arrange a meeting place for tonight?"

"Not yet," he said. "Why don't you meet me for lunch, and we can *fixe une rendezvous?*"

His easy transition to French was delightful, something she and Martin used to do: eat dinner in French, read Rilke *auf Deutsch*, sing Portuguese ballads like love-struck bohemian poets. She dressed hurriedly in a casual suit and over-the-knee boots and rushed downstairs to a cafe at the corner of Stephensplatz. Several minutes later Otto came toward her. He was taller than she remembered and carried a cardboard tube beneath his arm. Wind blew loose a red place mat. He snagged it from the air and then sat. While he studied the menu, she saw that his nose canted to one side, giving his face a pleasing asymmetry. The humidity had dropped, and he looked terribly healthy in his crisp, seersucker suit.

She agreed to the Riesling he proposed and ordered the first salad on the menu. The waiter returned with the wine and a silver cooler. Wine would be good, she thought. The concert would keep her up late. She could use a nap.

"You mentioned you'd visited the States," she said.

"After the war, I worked as a draftsman in New York."

"A draftsman! Do they have those anymore?"

"No. The whole profession has changed."

"When was this?"

"I went in '53 and came home in '58, then lived like a pauper on my wife's teaching salary. It was ten years until I received a commission." His eyes skipped across the parapets of buildings. "Vienna was rattling with pensioners and amputees. Now, it is a young person's city, and I am ready to retire."

"You look too young to retire," she said.

"I hike every weekend."

"I like to hike."

"Where?"

"The Adirondacks."

"Ah, the Adirondacks. I used to hike there, back in the days before ticks and Lyme disease."

"Why did you return to Austria?"

He turned toward the plaza. "To repair the rubble."

"But the city looks perfectly preserved."

"The façades are the same, but we architects made new everything within the historic shell of the past."

The shell of the past. Her skin tingled. She knew about that. "How wonderful. Respectful."

Eating her salad and drinking her wine, she thought, I am truly enjoying myself. Food. Conversation. How long it had been.

After the meal, Otto walked her back to the pension.

"So, shall I pick you up here?" Otto said.

"Thank you, no. I need time to gather myself. I'll see you at the venue."

COUGHS RICOCHETED THROUGH the hall. The orchestra shimmered in the bright rectangle of the stage. Neva, a white swan in red satin and diamonds, came down the aisle to the front row. Otto, in a tuxedo, had arrived early. He stood and greeted her with a bow and extended a hand to help her to her seat. She knew they made a handsome couple and couldn't help a glowing smile.

The choir, dressed in burgundy robes, filled the risers. Herr Lautner strode across the stage, tuxedo tails flapping, hair slicked back with pomade. Stepping onto the podium, he raised his baton.

The choral piece, "Falling in Flight," began with the brass establishing a theme of rising fourths and fifths, speaking directly to the musical subconscious. One by one the woodwinds, strings, and voices joined, a happy jamboree of sound with a single, underlying conversation. Neva had written the score without measures and marked each musician's sheet music "count to ten" or "count to five." Her music went to the very core of the musicians' art, natural breathing and a sense of phrasing. A professional, especially a Viennese, was more than an instrument with a foot tapping out 4/4 time. As she watched the conductor, she felt an intense longing to direct her own piece, to wade hip deep in the ocean, making herself vulnerable to the next big wave of sound. She wanted to be knocked flat.

When the harmonics changed, the tenors, altos and sopranos assembled in the layered *oohming* of Tibetan monks. *Wow, wow, wow* vibrated through the Grand Saal. Bringing both arms down in a violent thrash, the conductor halted all sound. In the silence, the air rang with a tinny, whispered vibration. So far, so good, she thought, nearly euphoric that the tricky middle had gone well. Settling against the seat, she slid her elbow back on the armrest and felt Otto's shoulder. Not wanting to be distracted she pulled away.

In the final third the strings and voices traded chants, calling across a chasm. To her horror, Herr Lautner's arms jerked up and down. The freewheeling tumble stopped. The orchestra marched to his tempo.

The end stunk. There was applause, appreciative but not a roar.

Otto clapped heartily. "*Sehr gut! Wunderbar!*"

"*Danke,*" she said, acknowledging the false praise.

The disappointing end took her back to Martin's funeral, the dim yellow light filtering through the shades, the flowers shedding seeds across her desk. While her mother and sister fielded phone calls from friends and colleagues, Neva sat at her desk with the score of *Figaro* propped against the wall.

But this performance had none of Puccini's sparkle. Her composition was flawed. She had feared it. Now she knew, and she must face the final humiliation: congratulating the conductor.

AT THE RECEPTION, the prongs of Otto's fingers steered her through women in evening dress, beaded bags clutched to their bosoms, and tuxedoed instrumentalists sipping champagne. This happy clamor was the effect she'd wanted. As she approached the conductor, he looked her up and down.

"Frau Roth, delighted you could join us." Herr Lautner nodded at a ring of men. "I believe you know everyone?"

The head of the Music School, Herr Dr. Witz, whose mustache style had surely been lifted from the era of Franz Josef, offered his congratulations. He gave a sideways glance at the conductor. "Very challenging piece."

"The idea came from Puccini," she said.

"Yes?" said Witz. "I would have thought Britten or your famous Eastern influence."

"No gamelans," she said. "No ten-tone scale."

She looked around for the Schoenberg's Music Director, an ally, but he had disappeared into the cliques of mostly grayhaired men. By God, was she going to have to justify her composition? Yes, she was, and she would.

"The balance between abandon and control—"

"Ah yes, the *converso* of Puccini," Otto chimed in. "One cannot praise him too much." He pinched her arm and locked his hand around her elbow.

She glared at him and shook free. "As I was saying before you interrupted me," — she turned back to the gaggle of critics — "the switchbacks need the proper balance between abandon and control."

Herr Lautner accepted a glass of champagne. "Perhaps you place too much responsibility on the musicians."

"Not at all. The musicians can feel the descant build." She made a fist and beat three times against her chest. "Music *must* come from the core."

AFTERWARDS, SHE REFUSED to take Otto's arm. Fog from the Danube had settled over the city. Mist glazed the cobblestones and muffled the clip-clop of carriage horses. Despite that, the night was pleasant and warm. She walked with her arms folded over her chest and a clutch tucked beneath her arm.

"Why on earth did you pinch me?"

"You were angry," he said.

"So?"

Otto laughed. "I have known well one other hotheaded woman, and I find it *wunderbar* that you do not disguise your feelings. With such a woman, one always knows where one stands. But in the end, was it not better to flare at me than at Lautner?" He cocked his head and smiled.

Streetlamps sculpted the squared planes of his broad forehead and high cheekbones. Was there something hidden and rigid about him?

"So, tell me about your wife." Her own kind of verbal pinch.

"My wife is no more."

A German idiom for death. *Ist nicht mehr.*

Oh, poor man. "When did you lose her?"

"Four years ago." He pulled his chin. "No. Four and a half."

"My husband has been dead a year," she said.

"*Ach so?*"

"His parents came from Vienna."

"What did he do?"

"Martin was a math professor at Columbia."

"Were you happy?"

"Very."

He nodded solemnly. "Then you have a long path ahead."

He offered his elbow and she took it. Restaurant awnings had been rolled up. Barrel-backed chairs faced each other across empty tables. Shutters on the upper floors had been closed against the damp.

"Did you find it hard to get on with your life?"

"Certainly," he said, "but I told myself it was the same after the war. Time passes and one tries to construct a life alone."

"And you're all right?"

"Life is for the living."

"My husband is the only person on earth who truly understood me."

"Once, I would have said the same, but I find now that I can have a good understanding with many more than I imagined. So to say, friends of the heart, *nicht wahr?*"

She wanted to ask him more about how he had managed to reconstitute his life, for it was something she knew she should do. Her life had devolved into a list of "shoulds". Clean out Martin's closet. Go over to Columbia and arrange for an archivist to comb through his papers. Sit down with an accountant and see where she stood for next year's taxes.

All too quickly, they had arrived back at the pension. She turned to face him, and though she was tall, he was taller. Had she known him better, she might have given in to her impulse to rest her head on his shoulder. Instead, she extended a hand.

"This has been very helpful, Otto. Since my husband's death, I feel my spirit being crushed beneath a mountain of emotionally draining tasks."

"Then while you are here, you must have some fun. Perhaps you can go home with some energy to tackle what you must." He placed a hand on her shoulder. "Are you still willing for me to play tour guide?"

"Promise I don't have to be in a good mood."

"Not for me. I have my bad days, too."

THE NEXT DAY he informed her that their first stop was a short subway ride away. No one could leave Vienna without seeing the Kunsthistorisches Museum.

"My husband's parents always talked about that." Art history professors, they had emigrated to America two years before the *Anschluss*. Martin's dear, dear parents. Gone, too.

And here she was, still smarting from last night's debacle, standing in a room of Flemish miniatures. The museum was famous for its early Renaissance landscapes. Farmlands. Windmills. Dark skies.

Hands clasped behind his back, Otto leaned past the stanchions and rope that kept visitors from getting too close. An alarm sounded. She pulled him back. A guard hurried toward them.

Otto held up his hands.

After issuing a warning, the guard returned to an adjoining room. Neva burst into laughter and then clamped a hand over her mouth.

Otto, laughing, too, looked around guiltily. "Did that make you nervous?"

"Well, I don't want my tour guide to get arrested."

"I only look. Never touch. However, let me show you the benefit of standing close."

He beckoned her toward the portrait of a cow, and when she stood as close as he wanted her to, details leapt out — wet nostrils; individual eyelashes; dolorous eyes. All totally realistic. All temptingly touchable — but *not*.

"It's the portrait of a soul," she said.

"*Genau!*"

She had passed the test.

"What's on the agenda for the rest of the day?"

After the museum and lunch, he proposed a concert at the cathedral. Tickets had already been purchased, so there was no sense her begging off.

"Organ concerts are my favorite," she said. "How did you guess?"

"Your every wish is my desire," he said with a wink and a bow.

She smiled. "My every wish is your command. That's the way we say it."

"I don't like to command. I would rather persuade."

THE CROWD SURGED through the massive wooden doors of St. Stephen's. Inside, a breeze swept through the nave and out the clerestory windows. A bird slapped the wooden beams. She hoped it wasn't trapped. As concertgoers found their seats, all was commotion. The cathedral, where the great "Papa Haydn" had served as Kapellmeister, was chock-a-block with heavy, carved wood. She felt small and insignificant, her music, and even her recent inability to compose, diminished by the old man's genius.

When she slid into a pew, her leg pressed Otto's thigh. He glanced down, then placed an arm around her shoulder. She shivered with pleasure.

A thousand voices gabbled. She took a blank staff book from her purse.

"How do you write music?" he said.

"I start by thinking of the piece as a table — square, round, oval-shaped — with leaves or without."

"Such a domestic image!"

"In most ways I am a very traditional woman."

His thumb dug into a knot on her neck.

Relax, she told herself. "Thanks," she said. "That feels good."

He placed a hand on her knee. "And about the music?"

What had he asked? All this contact. All this touching. Oh, yes, about how she composed.

"Let's say I get a commission for a piece forty-five-minutes long. I imagine an oval-shaped table with no leaves. In the be-ginning the table is covered with a lace tablecloth. I can see the dark color of the wood underneath, but nothing of the grain. I have only a sense of the size and shape of the composition. Then, if the patron tells me what feeling the piece should have, I search for the same feeling in myself."

"What do you do once you know the feeling?"

"I make little rips in the tablecloth, here and here and here." With her fingernails, she opened imaginary holes. "To expose bits of wood grain. I begin to see a pattern. I connect the larger holes. Finally, I have a composition."

"This delights me," he said. "Our creative process is very similar."

"Oh?"

From an inside pocket, he withdrew a mechanical pencil. "May I borrow your notebook?"

"Just until the concert starts."

He glanced at the nearby oratory, an elevated crow's nest reached by a winding stair. His pencil drew a vine around the edge of the page. He turned the line into a banister. Frogs with inward turning toes squatted on the rail.

She looked from the drawing to the banister.

"I didn't see the froggies until you drew them," she said.

"As with music, details suggest the whole."

Moved that he had grasped so quickly the thing that meant the most to her in life, she touched her fingers lightly to her throat.

A murmur traveled through the crowd. Heads craned, looking toward the organist, whose keyboard at the side of the cathedral suddenly sparkled with a pinpoint of light. The first, heavy chords of the Baroque organ rang out. Bach's powerful B-minor Toccata resembled a medieval tapestry, notes in high registers weaving, like whites and yellows, through the mighty purple bass. She allowed the music to press upon her heart and shorten her breath. Tears flowed freely.

Otto handed her a handkerchief and dabbed his own eyes with his thumbs.

Then it was over. The audience burst into applause.

"I hope it wasn't too much," he said.

"Oh, no!" she said. "It was cathartic. It emptied me out."

Otto looked ahead at the tabernacle. "The B-minor Toccata was my wife's favorite, and this was an extraordinary performance."

Unlike last night, she thought. But never mind. No point dwelling on that.

Near the exit he pulled her out of the shuffling crowd. "Wait. Look here."

Display cases on the transept wall held old newspaper articles and black-and-white photographs. In the images, she saw that the nave of St. Stephen's, where the bird had been flying, had once stood open to the sky. There were blocks of rubble. Crushed pews. Shattered glass.

He put his finger on the single, standing arch. "This was all we had to work with. This *nothing*."

She looked up at the high vaults. "How on earth did you put it all back?"

"Stone by stone. The same way I rebuilt my life."

"I wish I could believe that were possible. Since my husband's death I have had no musical ideas. I don't know if I'll ever write again."

"I hope you will." He took her arm and led her toward the door.

Across from the eastern portal of the cathedral, a pyramid of glass bombarded the plaza with brassy light. Neva shielded her eyes.

He stepped between her and the glare. "Earlier, I had an idea."

"What kind of idea?" She pulled large black sunglasses

from her clutch. Now she could think without worry of being blinded.

"Would you consider writing a commissioned piece for a women's choral group here in Vienna?"

"Not the Schoenberg Choir?"

"The Frauengesang Verein."

"Is it for some occasion?"

"An anniversary," he said. "I am on the Board."

"Who is the client really? Is there a Music Director, or will I have to please the whole Board, an impossible task, I might add. I've tried before."

"I am the client," said Otto. "You have only me to please."

She slipped off her sunglasses. "You can't be serious."

"Indeed, I am."

The sun fell behind the roofs. If she landed a new commission, maybe that would get the creative juices flowing. The pension was but a short walk across the square, and these preliminary negotiations generally took time.

"Tell me more about the group," she said.

"It's a women's choir of mature voices."

"An experienced choral group, then?"

"Why don't you judge for yourself? These people are my dearest friends, and tonight we meet for dinner in Grinzing. Besides," he added, giving her a wink, "they might join in sponsoring the commission."

"Oh, good. I can raise my fee."

"So you will do it?"

"Let's see how things go."

If she was meeting Otto's friends, she needed to shower and change clothes.

"One more question," she said. "How exactly were you able to get on with your life?"

"I had no choice."

"Do you date?"

"I think of it more as developing friendships." He pushed open the pension's filigreed door. "My wife always arranged our free time. If I made no effort, I would find myself sitting home every night. Is it not pleasant to enjoy the company of the opposite sex?"

She made herself exhale. "Yes, certainly."

He insisted on accompanying her in the elevator. On the sixth floor, just as she was about to insert the key, he took it from her. "Before we go in, I have something to ask. Did you bring the red scarf you wore in Salzburg?"

A shawl, not a scarf. "You remember what I wore?"

"You had on slim black pants."

"Shouldn't I wear something more formal?"

"Not at all. Be yourself."

"Are you going to leave and come back?"

"No, I'll wait in the breakfast room."

"All right," she said.

He opened the door and stood aside, letting her enter.

In her room she saw that the maid had folded Martin's nightshirt and placed it on a pillow. She pressed it against her cheek and consigned it to her suitcase. Just in case.

She showered and put on pants and heels. Surely, they'd done enough walking for the day. And if she was to do a commission for this group, she wanted to look her best. The tassels of her shawl swung as she trotted down the hall.

"Beautiful," Otto said. "A work of art." Rather than a cab, he suggested the *Strassenbahn*.

How comfortable he seemed with his life as presently constituted. If only she could get there.

THE TRACKS QUIVERED and sang. "What is this Grinzing place?" she asked, looking out at the houses with their

155

window boxes of red and white geraniums.

"So to explain to you, Grinzing is where Beethoven composed his *Pastorale*. Mahler is buried in the graveyard."

"Should I have brought a bouquet?"

"We can let the graveyard alone."

A bittersweet laugh. "Yes, I have had quite enough of graveyards."

The connection with Beethoven and Mahler had Neva expecting a grand Schloss. But, no. Grinzing was a modest village of stucco farmhouses, vineyards spreading beyond the edge of town.

The streetcar stopped, and he helped her down the steps.

"Despite its distance from the city, quite a lot of tourists come here," he said.

"To look at Mahler's grave?"

"For the *heuriger* wine."

"I don't know that word."

"It is wine from the new harvest, similar to France's Beaujolais *nouveau*." He pinched his thumb and index finger. "A bit sour, some say."

"I hate sweet wine."

"So, no Mogan David?"

"That especially."

"Reserve your verdict." Saying something about wreaths and landmarks, Otto set off down the village street.

Cobblestones caught her heels. She'd been thinking about the commission, not practical shoes.

"Wait up!" she called.

He halted immediately, looking around as if lost. "I was trying to recall where Beethoven lived."

"What am I, your subservient little Japanese wife?"

He walked back and offered his arm. "Without a woman's civilizing influence, we men forget our manners."

She tried to keep the weight on the balls of her feet. "I wish I'd worn tennies."

He slipped an arm around her waist. "If you stumble I will catch you."

She smiled. "You have impeccable manners."

Besides, he made a handsome escort. For two blocks, passing a dozen wineries, she let herself be carried along by his company and the smoky aroma of meat cooked on a rotisserie, and she began to wish that something, not yet daring to be named, could develop from smiles and touches.

Finally, he steered her through an arch wide enough for a horse-drawn wagon. A courtyard furnished with two dozen picnic tables opened before her.

"Here we are!" Otto announced.

Austrian men in business suits and women in aproned *dirndls* hoisted empty pitchers at passing waiters. A stocky man in a green felt country jacket stood and waved. Missing a step, Neva tripped.

"*Oopsala!*" Otto caught her under the arms.

Neva straightened herself, but when she looked over at the table, she saw that the smiles had dropped from the faces of the women. They looked her up and down, seemingly taking her measure. The evening was either very warm, or the prickly sensation on her cheeks meant her face was turning red, just when she wanted to come across as cool and assured.

"*Meine Damen und Herren,*" Otto said to the group, "it is my honor to present to you the famous American composer Neva Roth."

Neva's scarlet shawl slipped from her shoulders. She busied herself retying the knot so that she did not have to respond to the up-and-down assessments of the men. Looking like Audrey Hepburn in her black turtleneck and stretch pants, she'd already seen that she was a hundred pounds lighter and ten years younger than anyone else. Why had she come out here with a man she barely knew?

Otto seated her next to a Frau Schmidt. After a sidelong glance, Frau Schmidt spoke in a guttural Austrian dialect to the woman opposite, her hair a stiff meringue. If Neva was to have any standing with these people, she would have to jump into the conversation.

"I understand that you and Herr Hoffmann are old friends."

Frau Schmidt turned, drawing her elbows in. "Do you speak German?"

"Yes," Neva said.

Frau Schmidt switched to *Hoch Deutsch*. "Then we can't say bad things about you, can we?"

The other women laughed.

Neva was in no mood to be the butt of their jokes, but knew it would be more diplomatic to deflect. "Do you sing with the Frauengesang Verein?"

"Once I did." Frau Schmidt refilled her wine glass. "Now my voice cracks."

"Could you tell me how large the group is?"

"Eighty, plus or minus."

"Are the singers trained?"

"Since we were children, we all sang together." Frau Schmidt drew a circle in the air to incorporate all the tables. "This group here."

She pointed out who sang which parts in the chorus, when they had joined and when retired. The quality of Frau Schmidt's voice, sharp even in speech, and the gossipy manner in which she raked over each singer's flaws, reminded Neva how much she disliked catty women.

The man in the green coat stood. Otto removed his tie and stuffed it in his pocket. He squeezed Neva's thigh. "Don't disappear."

When he left, Frau Schmidt said in a stage whisper, "Don't pay any attention to Otto. He's just lonely."

Frankly, Neva wasn't sure *what* she felt. Off balance, perhaps.

"We didn't realize you really were a composer," said the woman with the white bouffant. "Greta here. Pleased to meet you." She reached across the table, offering a hand.

Neva shook it. "A pleasure."

A woman in an unfortunate lilac pantsuit moved closer. "We thought you were another one of Otto's women."

"'Otto's women?'" Neva said.

"I don't blame him," said Frau Schmidt.

"Blame him for what?" Neva asked, keeping a stone face and disinterested tone.

"For taking companions," said the woman in lilac, frowning at Neva as though she were a dimwit.

The need for companionship Neva knew well, and she did not blame Otto for beginning to date. Four years was a long time.

"We went to school with Hildi," said the woman with the hair.

"Yes," said Frau Schmidt, "and she does not recognize any of us."

"You mean *did*, do you not?" Neva said.

Frau Schmidt's heavy eyebrows drew together. "She's still alive. In body."

Neva looked from one to the other. Smiles dropped from their faces.

"Does she have…Is she in a…"

"Home for Alzheimer's?" Frau Schmidt said. "Yes, and for a time when we visited, we could get her to remember our school days. But now? Nothing at all."

"She sits in a wheelchair and whimpers," said the woman

with curls, "and at night she screams."

"Otto can hardly stand to visit," Frau Schmidt said.

"And you remain his friends?"

Frau Schmidt shrugged. "We have many widows in our circle, and they say he is never disloyal to his wife."

"Do you understand?" asked the woman in lilac.

Neva understood all right. Look, but don't touch. He didn't
have sex.

Through an open door she saw him in a line of men, arms
crossed, laughing with the other men. His wife was alive. He
could sit with her, touch her hand, talk to her. Even if she did
not talk back, she was alive, poor woman.

And here was Neva with her tight clothes and red scarf, her
movie-star glasses in her clutch, looking to these peasants like a
modern-day Carmen, or worse, Jezebel.

Carrying two plates, Otto returned. When he lowered hers
into view, she gasped at the pile of heavy Austrian fare. Thick
slabs of bacon. Nockerl dumplings. Two scoops of potato salad.

No wonder the women were fat. The breeze shifted, and a
barnyard smell blanketed the patio.

Frau Schmidt sniffed. "What reeks?"

Yes, indeed. Something was rotten in the state of Denmark,
Neva thought.

Otto placed a hand on her shoulder. Mr. Touchy-Feely.

"You must eat," he said.

She was surrounded by Aryans. "I can't eat this."

"Why not?"

"Jews don't eat pork as you undoubtedly know without me
telling you."

She cupped her hands around her face. Please don't cry, she
thought. Whatever you do, don't make a scene. She threw a leg
over the bench. If she could just get some air. He grabbed her
arm, but she twisted away, removed her heels, and bolted bare-

foot through the arch and out to the street, running downhill toward the streetcar stop. Otto caught up just as the streetcar, its bell ringing, opened its doors.

She took a window seat and pulled the shawl over her head. Otto slid in next to her.

The streetcar was stuffy and overheated. She threw off the shawl and tried opening the window. Unable to budge it, she beat the glass with her fists.

"Calm *down*." Otto stood and forced the latch.

As the wind whipped her hair, she convinced herself that no man would ever be able to stand her again; she would be miserably alone the rest of her life. She crushed the shawl to her eyes and hunched over, elbows on her knees.

Half an hour until they reached the city proper. She would ignore the barricade of his crossed arms. She could endure it. This situation was minor, compared to the other things she had endured. This was very nearly comical.

HE HADN'T SAID a word the whole way back, and then he stood. "Our stop is the next."

"It's not *our* stop. It's *my* stop." If he tried to touch her, she would sock him.

But he did not.

At the pension he took out a euro for the elevator.

She started for the spiral stairs.

"As you wish, *Gnädige Frau*, but I take the elevator."

The marble treads felt good on her bare feet. "I need the exercise."

The elevator rose alongside her. Otto stood in the cubicle as she circled the shaft. On the third floor, she stopped to catch her breath.

The platform lifted his feet above her head, and he called down. "We did not have time to discuss the commission."

"Oh, that."

"Yes, that," he said.

The elevator's light cast moving shadows along the wall. The elevator clanged to a halt.

Winded and in need of a hot bath, she arrived on the sixth floor.

Otto moved slowly from the shadows. "We must talk."

"I'm not doing the music, Herr Hoffmann. I can't." She tried to slip past him. Get her key in the lock. The day had done her in.

He took her key and closed his fingers around it. "Please," he said. "This anniversary will come only once."

"Find the Frauen whatever another composer."

"You misunderstand," he said. "It is not for them."

"Isn't it for their anniversary?"

"It is for mine," he said. "The fiftieth of my wedding. The golden one."

The hall light clicked off automatically, plunging her into darkness. With a blood-curdling scream, the gears of the ancient elevator engaged. Standing very near the stairs, she found herself resisting the downward suck of air and the clank and hiss of a cable lowering the elevator to the lobby. She reached in the darkness for Otto's hand, surprising herself. He caught her wrist and pressed her hand to his heart, his breathing that of a man laboring under a heavy load. He wore a subtle pine cologne, and it was that, as much as anything, that made her slip her arms around his waist. Hugging him was like hugging a tree: straight, solid, resinous. The cashmere of his sweater caressed her cheek. How much time did he have? How much time did she?

"I thought we both were widowed," she said.

"The wife I knew is dead, and I would throw myself at your feet if I thought it would convince you to undertake my commission. I want a memorial to show how marriage makes a common history. I had hoped to give you some idea of what my wife was like before the disease. Her friends have memories I do not."

"But I ran out."

"It was not because you are Jewish."

Neva drew back. His face blurred in the dark.

"I ran because you are not free."

A spasm passed down his body. "And you are."

He stepped back, one relationship between them extinguished, the other, as client and patron, still possible.

"I so hope — I pray — you can make my idea a reality."

"I'm sorry, Herr Hoffmann. I truly can't."

"Well, then." He clicked his heels and bowed. Clutching the iron rail, he started down the stairs.

Neva listened to the diminuendo of his steps.

Back in the room she dropped her shoes by the door Her notebook lay where she had tossed it on the bed. She pulled a chair to the desk and turned on the lamp. Like the illustration on an illuminated manuscript, Otto's drawing twined around the border of the page. Treble notes filled the staffs. Could she actually have started something new?

She flipped the page. Not Bach, exactly, but a theme. She opened a drawer and found a pen. Around and through Otto's drawing, she parted the lace. The sound of "wedding" sprang from the page, the beginning of love and its end.

She heard voices singing.

YEAR BY YEAR

———o———

S HE'S FINE WITH the hearing aids, perfectly safe, and for all Klara Schmidt cares, her children can walk in and find her dead. An army of two, they have mobilized to move her from her home. She looks through the filmy curtains to the patio where Rolf, a lumpen shadow, thumbs through the money in his wallet. A man in overalls, walking backwards, wheels away her Weber grill. Rolf opens the patio's sliding door, slams it, and drops the wooden dowel in the metal track. He swipes a handkerchief across his forehead and wrings his whisk-broom beard.

"What you up to there, *Mutti?*"

"Mending your socks," she says.

Her sewing basket sits on the coffee table. As she slides her grandmother's darning egg, a smooth onyx oval, into the sock's worn toe, she remembers the dear woman's half-moon glasses and fingers, twisted but adept, stabbing at the handiwork. Klara threads her needle, knots the thread, and bites it off.

Already her son is pinning on his CVS badge.

ROLF SCHMIDT
ASST. MANAGER

So proud of so little.

Her needle makes another pass. "What did he give you for the barbecue?"

Straightening the name tag, Rolf's hand freezes. He looks at the ceiling, and his tongue pushes out his cheek. It was his "tell" — a physical indication of his lying.

"A fin," he says.

"A dorsal fin?" she says.

"Very funny, Ma." He takes out his wallet and puts a five-dollar bill on her sewing basket.

She picks up the money and tucks it in her bra. He's lying, of course. He got more.

The big ring of keys clipped to his belt jingles. Her son stands like a bull terrier. "In half an hour a guy's coming by to look at that old radio," Rolf shouts. "Think you can handle it?"

Without looking up from her task, she touches an ear. "I have my hearing aids."

"I forgot," he says.

"I hear everything, good as new." If he could lie, so could she. She had lost one of the hearing aids, and before her daughter arrives, she needs to find it.

Rolf frowns, hesitates, and after dislodging the dowel, opens the patio door. "I'll take a chair to the garage." He picks up a plastic chair he'd brought over from the drugstore: six bucks, after his employee's discount. "That way, you can keep a lookout."

Keep a lookout. It reminds her of when he played Cowboys and Indians. He doesn't trust her to hear the doorbell.

"How much am I asking for the radio?" she says.

"A hundred twenty," he says. "No less than a hundred. Cheap jerks always want to haggle."

Eckhart would hate the radio being sold.

"A hundred's not much. I keep it then."

"What do you want that old thing for?"

She makes another pass across the darning egg and draws together the hole's frayed edges. "I take it with me to your house."

"Don't do this to me, *Mutti*. We've been over this a million times."

"I don't make trouble for no one."

"That's not the point. It's just that St. Paul's Home is such a nice place. You'll have beautiful meals." He bends to kiss the top of her head. "Your social life's going to improve a thousand percent."

"I don't want to live with strangers."

Rolf looks impatiently at his watch. Digital. Another deal from the store. "You'll make new friends."

"At my age you don't make friends," Klara says. "You bury them." Klara lets her glasses slide down her nose. "I'm not going. I've made up my mind and that is all."

"You better talk to Marlies," he says.

"I am not incompetent."

"But, *Mutti*—"

The phone interrupts him. Half the time it's telemarketers, but just in case. She puts aside her sewing and knuckles off the couch.

"Want me to get that?" Rolf says.

"Yes," she says.

He rushes toward the kitchen, says hello, and hands the phone around the kitchen door. "It's Gisela."

Her niece from Germany. She takes the receiver. "*Hallo! Klara Schmidt here.*"

"Auntie Klara!" her niece shouts. "So good to hear you."

"It is not necessary to raise your voice." Klara switches the receiver to her other ear. The hearing in her left is slightly better than her right. Ever since Klara's twin moved to the new place, Gisela has initiated their monthly call from her cell phone, and

Klara has told her niece about her hearing aids and her hope that she will not have to move the way her sister did. There on the refrigerator under that magnetic banana is a brochure from Zelda's retirement home, a three-story brick building with a columned portico that looks like the ones at fancy hotels. There is a photo of Zelda in her room. Behind her overstuffed chair, lace curtains hang, and the rose-colored carpet looks new. Her twin has a wicked smile. Even so, Klara is ashamed that Zelda, the daring one, the one who never asked permission, has finally given in to her children's demands.

"Can you put your mother on?" Klara says. "I want to discuss our birthday celebration."

"I'm calling from my house," Gisela says.

"What's wrong?" Klara says. "Is everything all right?"

"Mom's not feeling well."

Rolf pushes Klara aside and opens the door to the garage. Hot, humid air balloons into her kitchen. Rolf carries the plastic chair to the garage and then points from his wristwatch to his chest. His fingers make a walking motion, he smiles and makes a thumbs up, and then closes the door.

"What are you telling me?" Klara says. "Rolf was here bothering me, but he just went out."

"I was saying that Mom gave us a scare last week," Gisela says, "but now she's stabilized."

"What means this 'stabilized'?" Klara says.

"She's better," Gisela says.

"Tell her I'm coming," Klara says. If anything were seriously wrong with her sister, Klara would know it, the way she knew Eckhart had died, even before rolling over.

WHEN SHE STEPS down into the garage, all but empty thanks to Rolf, the humidity makes her gasp. Apart from the steel shelving, what's left is Eckhart's workbench: maple-topped, fourteen feet long, with a wood vise and a steel one. Marlies's son Gary, who did four tours of duty in Afghanistan, wants the workbench. "Gramps would like it if we kept it in the family," he told her. Forty-two, unemployed, Gary is the only person who ever drops by without calling, the only one who sits and visits. His hobby is remote-controlled model planes. He brought one he had completed to show her. It came in a kit. He brought the box, too.

She sits in the plastic chair, fanning herself with a fly swatter, and looks out at the street where two girls, their hair in pigtails, glide backwards on rubber-wheeled skates. They live on the corner. A few years back Klara bought Kool-Aid from a table they'd set up in their yard. Now, they are at a gawky, high-spirited age and so caught up in executing turns they can't be bothered to wave. "Don't be such fidgeters!" Klara's mother used to say, and for no reason, except that Klara and her sister swung their feet at the table.

Almost like a family member, the radio — Violetta, this model's name — looks down from a shelf. The radio is a Tonfunk, a masterpiece of German electronics. It is rectangular and about the size of a toaster oven. Over the decades the radio's gold brocade has turned the color of dark lager. A thin layer of dust covers the walnut case; the seven ivory, preset buttons are spaced like teeth. Klara remembers perching on a metal stool in the garage, listening to Schubert, while Eckhart's long legs poked out from beneath one of their Fords. Violetta was new then, along with her customs papers, wiring diagram, and boxes of fuses. Violetta is priceless. Violetta is a keeper.

The girls skate off.

In the driveway stands a middle-aged man with a basketball belly. He's wearing Carhartt overalls and a White Sox baseball cap, the bill stick-straight. His boots are worn down on the sides, giving him a shuffling walk, and he reminds Klara of the moon-faced Croats Eckhart used to work with at the shop.

He looks at a folded paper. "Is this the place for the radio?"

"You have it right," Klara says.

He scans the garage's empty shelves and the pegboards with their ghost outlines of wrenches. In the bed of his red pickup, the slats of a tall wooden fence contain used washers, bent siding, and storm doors.

"Looks like you're fixing to move," he says.

Fixing to. "Yes," she says. "I am fixing to move."

"Where you hiding the radio?"

Getting to her feet, she points to the shelf above the workbench.

"That's an old un, all right." He stabs a finger in Violetta's direction. "What's the hole in the radio? It looks like a car cigarette lighter."

The hole, on the left side of the radio, has always reminded Klara of a woman's eye looking out from behind a veil. On the Tonfunk brochure, the hole doesn't look that big, but the hole is what makes this model special. Klara spreads the brochure on the workbench to show him Violetta's features. "It is the first ever remote control," she says. "The radio turns on if you whistle at it."

She points to an illustration on the brochure. A hand holds a Bakelite whistle. From it, sound beams arc toward the hole.

"The original whistle fell off the workbench and shattered," she said, "but she'll turn on with a regular whistle."

"But does the radio work? I don't want it if the sound's messed up."

"It works fine."

A week ago, Rolf had climbed up and tested the buttons. None stuck. The speakers sounded good as new. She pulls open the tool bench's center drawer. The whistle is attached to a beaded lamp chain. When she blows, the radio does not turn on.

"One must blow a certain way, like calling a dog," she says.

"Let me give it a try." He holds out his hand.

He blows with all his might and the whistle peeps. The man has obviously never blown a whistle before.

Frowning, he plops the whistle on the bench. "Looks like she's a goner."

"If you reach, you can turn it on by hand." The only reason she is even bothering with this idiot is that extra cash for her trip would come in handy. She opens a steel cupboard where the vacuum tubes, all but those Eckhart replaced, stand neatly stacked in their slim, cardboard boxes: ECC85, ECH81, EF89, and EL84. "Look here. All original."

He raises his eyebrows, reconsidering.

"You take it from the shelf, you see it is fine," she says.

"Have you got a ladder?"

She shows him the plastic chair. "Only that."

"I saw your ad and thought maybe I could turn it at a swap meet, but not if it don't work. If you can't get rid of it, just put it in the alley."

"I never put her in the alley."

"Suit yourself. I know how it is when you're closing up shop."

Not possible. No one knew. Klara does not know herself.

When he is gone, she lowers the garage door. Enough with this garage sale. She picks up the whistle, and with a Kleenex, wipes off his germs. Blowing softly, she hears the whistle rattle. She blows harder until black dots float before her eyes, and when she looks up, Violetta's ivory teeth glow. The radio is on. Rolf must have lowered the volume. Without a step stool, the only way to shut off the radio is to pull the plug, and so she does.

BEFORE MARLIES ARRIVES, Klara must find that other hearing aid. She picks up the hearing aid case from the end table next to the couch. She removes the box's blue velvet liner. Not there. Having just one hearing aid is like driving with one head lamp, not that her kids would let her do that either. They took away her car keys.

Klara pads down the hall and flips back the clothes hamper's pink wooden lid. Flannel nightgown. Cotton panties. Chenille robe. A musty towel. She can almost remember the hard plastic peanut in the palm of her hand. She must have dozed off while watching television. Back in the living room, she digs around in the couch cushions and finds nothing but hairpins and lint. Fifty-three cents, likely from Rolf's pants.

Usually she starts the day with an hour of floor exercise, which is why she can still get down on all fours. Crawling like a potato farmer, she pushes her fingers through the shag carpet. Any moment, the plastic hearing aid will dig into her knee. And, she'd better find it. She has this trip to Germany coming up, their ninetieth birthday celebration, and she will need to be sociable with Zelda's guests.

Where, oh where, could it be? Klara sits on the couch trying to reconstruct yesterday's movements. Her shower. Some sewing. But there's nothing in the sewing basket — she already checked — and she has a fluttery feeling made up of guilt and shame, a feeling she remembers from childhood, the moment just before getting caught in a lie.

Just then Marlies breezes in the front door, the gust of humid air blowing across the living room to the filmy curtains that cover the sliding doors. With a wave and a nod of her head, Klara's daughter kicks the door shut. Marlies carries in half a dozen disassembled wardrobe boxes, which she props against the planter. Shortly after Klara and her husband bought the house, Eckhart built a waist-high planter to shield the living room from these air blasts. In the year since his death — has it been a year already? — Klara has given up on the ivy. Crispy dead, it stubbornly clings to the white lattice that extends to the ceiling.

Her daughter, still wearing her Cut' N' Curl's pink smock, heads toward the bedrooms. Each visit feels like an inspection because it is. Pills laid out in the blue plastic box on the counter. Bath checked for signs that she has showered. Walking down the hall where her daughter has not bothered to turn on the light because she knows Klara doesn't waste electricity, she sees Marlies race up from the basement with a plastic storage bin. She's taking it to the room set up for German visitors. Six-ty-one, Marlies still calls it "my room".

Behind Klara, a muffled thump sounds like boxes falling. With her knees smarting from rug burns, Klara hobbles back to the entry. Marlies's boxes are larger than card tables. Somehow, they slid down and wedged between the planter and front door.

"This is not a good place for your boxes," Klara calls.

"They're *your* boxes, not mine," Marlies shouts. "Don't wor-ry about it."

Her daughter so likes that expression. Also, "I can handle it." At one time, Klara had a notebook to record these Ameri-can sayings.

"I move the boxes if you are too busy," Klara calls.

"Don't, Ma. You'll hurt yourself."

Klara slides her fingers under the topmost box. It's heavy. If Marlies would come out here, she could see herself what the problem is. The three large boxes push at the planter. If it falls, the copper container of potting soil will spill on the living room rug, and Klara can't run the vacuum until she finds that hearing aid. It's these small things, one piled on another, that add to the widow's knot bowing her spine.

IN THE BACK bedroom, Marlies, sorting through the contents of the box from the basement, sits straddle-legged on a corner the bed. Her hair has thinned. She uses Dixie-Peach to spike the top.

"Do you think we could have some light on the subject?" Marlies asks.

Klara presses her lips together and thrusts her hands in her apron pockets.

"C'mon, Ma. It's like a tomb in here."

"It is only for not wasting the cooling."

Marlies snaps a leaf bag from a roll. Glad Bags. Not so glad, thinks Klara.

"If you want my help, then turn on the light or open the fucking blinds."

What is the good of saying, *I wish you wouldn't use that word?* Her daughter won't listen. Klara unhooks her hearing aid and takes it off.

Marlies takes the device from Klara and pushes it back in Klara's ear. "Why aren't you wearing both of them?"

Klara rubs the back of her ear. "It makes a *weh–weh*."

Smiling, Marlies says, "A *weh–weh*, huh? You used to say that when I skinned my knees." When Marlies sits back on the bed, its springs creak.

Klara reaches over her daughter's head to raise the blinds. Behind the steel barricade that blocks the dead end, sacks and papers have blown up against the wall of dry, uncut grass at the end of the cul-de-sac. Eckhart had given up on Chicago doing anything about the empty acres. He tilled the soil, leveled the ground with a lawn roller, and spread grass seed. Once a week he sprayed the baseball diamond with weed killer, though he stopped doing that when a neighbor complained about poison getting in the water supply. So now, tall weeds smother what had once been a patch of green. And still the City did nothing. But that was America. In Germany, a gardener would have mowed the weeds. A city gardener would have been trained in a school for gardeners. Here in America, no one got training, unless it was to go to war.

"St. Paul's called yesterday," Marlies said. "A spot's opened up, so that means we gotta make progress."

Progress. How to explain to Marlies that the objects in her house are not just objects. They are parts of her, as necessary as limbs. As skin. Without them, she is not sure how she will live.

Over Marlies's old desk hangs a shadow box: Schwalm embroidery. It's *Hessenstickerei*: her grandmother's needlework. "This flower bouquet is one your great-grandmother made," Klara says.

"Yeah, I know," Marlies says, not looking up.

Klara looks at the white-on-white woven basket. The flowers that spill out of it look exactly like a three-dimensional bouquet, but, in fact, the embroidered image is merely an illusion, nothing more than fabric and thread.

"Would you have a place for this?" Klara says.

"Put it on the bed," Marlies says. "I've still got all this shit to go through."

Klara carefully lifts the picture from the wall hanger and places it at the foot of the bed. The framed embroidery slides downhill and lodges against Marlies's fat-dimpled thigh.

Smirking, her daughter holds up a white gym suit with a flared skirt. "Size ten. Would you believe I could ever fit into this?"

"Are you taking some exercise?" Klara says.

"*Getting* some exercise," Marlies says.

Klara doesn't dare mention the word diet. Her daughter put on weight when she had babies and never took it off. Inside her suit of skin she carries an extra person.

Marlies stuffs the gym clothes in the open sack. "I should

go back to Nutri-system. Either that or get a divorce."

"What would you do?"

"Move to Arizona and buy a Harley."

"Would Josip move?"

"Not a chance."

"Are you making a joke?"

"No," Marlies says. "I'm completely serious. I hate my life."

"Gary's back," Klara says.

"That's what I'm talking about."

Ever since the Army sent Gary home, Marlies has spent most of her free time running Gary back and forth to the VA. Until recently, he wasn't able to drive himself, and it is a shame because he was the smart one, the one with the most ambition. Like Eckhart, he wanted to see the world.

Marlies opens the closet. "God damn! More boxes. What's all this?"

"Your things," Klara said. "I thought you would want them."

"Maybe." Marlies moves the boxes to the middle of the room and tears off more leaf bags.

"Do they think Gary's getting any better?" Klara says to her daughter's back.

"*Better?*" Marlies's head turns. "Honestly, Ma." Without a second look she stuffs high school yearbooks, spiral notebooks, and old binders into the trash. "I was reading this book on organization. I need to get a handle on how we're going to deal with all this crap. The guy says, handle everything once. Look at it. Remember why it was important. You're ready to pitch it then." Marlies collapses the box and shoves it under the bed. "We won't need these until we move you to the new place."

The new place. That is how her kids start talking when Klara objects to living with a bunch of Roman Catholics. She isn't Catholic, but Marlies married a Croat, and Klara knows how they are. Always wanting a priest to drop over.

She turns to leave the room. "How about I make a pot of coffee?"

"My ulcer's acting up," Marlies says. "How about you take down the pictures in the hall?"

"Fine," Klara says. "I do it."

"Bring all the pictures you want," Marlies says. "The one thing your new place has is plenty of wall space."

Even if Klara were going to St. Paul's, which she hopes, God willing, she can find some way to avoid, she wouldn't want to bring these reminders of time passing year by year. Not that she doesn't love her kids. They just didn't turn out the way she'd imagined. In the hall she pauses to look at a school picture of Rolf, a smiling boy with freckles and missing teeth. In Germany the school would have found a path for her boy: gardener, possibly. Auto mechanic. No, that would have been beyond him. Woodworker. Yes, he could have made furniture. He had been such a good boy at heart. Before taking the picture down, she touches her finger to the glass. *Auf wiedersehen.*

Moving down the gallery, she stops at a color portrait of Marlies. It is from one of those companies that used to send a photographer to your home. This is the way she likes to remember her daughter, her blonde little Marlies, a yellow ribbon in her hair. Klara's finger leaves a print on the glass. *Auf wiedersehen, Liebchen.*

"Move, Ma. I'm coming through," Marlies says.

Garbage bags over her shoulders, fingers hooked through the yellow cinch-ties, Marlies forces Klara back against the sanded plaster. The rough surface burns her elbows. No matter how fit she keeps herself, she can do nothing about the thinning skin.

Marlies turns. "And, oh, hey, Ma, that embroidery thing?"

"The *Hessenstickerei?*" Klara says.

"Two words. Craig's List!"

"Who is Craig? What list?"

Klara feels the vibration of a slammed door, but she does not hear Marlies's answer. Just as well. She wouldn't have liked it; and anyway, the pictures are heavy and breakable. She takes them to Marlies's room and lays them on the bed. Later, she can decide which are worth keeping and which the kids should take for themselves.

Coming back empty-handed, Marlies hefts one of the big wardrobe boxes and shoves it down the hall. "You might as well get going on this."

"On what?" Klara asks.

"Your clothes. Just pick out the ones you normally wear."

The box scoots past her and into her bedroom.

"So, I should stop with the pictures?" Klara says.

"Yes, stop. Let's work on the closet."

In the bedroom Klara slides open her closet. Five wool coats take up half of it. She doesn't wear just one. She wears them all, depending on the season.

"This is tiring," she says.

"Do you need to sit?" Marlies asks.

"I can keep going." It is not the standing so much as the decisions.

"Most of this stuff's just crap," Marlies says, "apart from Dad's tools. I hope Rolf's giving you the money."

"Oh, yes," Klara says.

On every visit, Klara sees the lines around her daughter's eyes, the temper that sent the wardrobe box scooting down the hall, never mind that it scratched the floor. Klara pulls the box into a parallelogram and stares at the drawing of how to fit the flaps. "Can you make this for me?"

"Sure." Marlies flips over the carton. Her daughter has this kind of ability, something Eckhart called spatial memory. When she graduated from high school, he wanted to bring her into the tool-and-die shop. Marlies's high school counselor encouraged her to go to beauty school, and Klara hopes it is the monotony of cutting hair all day and not a souring marriage that makes Marlies want to run away. Klara would give a fortune to see her daughter smile.

With the box assembled, Marlies flips it over. "Here you go."

Klara smells smoke on her daughter's breath. Not that again.

"I should tell you," Marlies says, "that the deposit on St. Paul's left you kind of low."

"How much is in my account?" Klara asks.

"Roughly $1200."

"I'll need some for Germany."

Marlies bends to pick up a sock. "Oh, well, that's fine then. You trot off to Germany and leave me to do all the work." Blinking back tears, Marlies runs her fingers through her hair. "This is going to take weeks to sort through."

Karla looks at the Ethan Allen bedroom suite and points to her dresser. "I want to take what's in there, and I will need this nightstand and light."

"That's it? That's all?"

Klara opens the closet. Hangers screech as she pushes aside all but the clothes she'll pack in her suitcase. It is much easier to think about what fits in a suitcase than to think what might fit in the closet at St. Paul's. The suitcase represents a place she wants to go, the closet, well, it is a permanent place. Her last place before the grave.

"Get rid of everything from here over."

"What about Dad's dresser?"

"Sell it," Klara says. "The only other thing I want is the radio in the garage."

Marlies gapes. "What about your TV and a living room chair?"

"Those, too."

Klara feels Marlies grasp her arms and peer closely in her face. "Are you feeling all right? I mean, you're not suicidal or anything."

"Why do you say that?"

"Gary, I guess. They say people start giving away their possessions after they've been moody and down, that's when you have to worry. I thought I was gonna have to drag you out of here."

"You won't," Klara says.

"You're not going to change your mind," Marlies says. " 'Cause when that estate agent comes, it's all going, whether you're here or not."

Klara takes a deep breath. A trip home. Time with her sister. Her life is moving forward again. "I don't know who will want all this, but they are welcome to it."

Klara feels herself gathered into her daughter's pillowy embrace. "Thank you, Ma. All of a sudden, the world is a brighter place."

FINALLY, KLARA IS on a plane. She has come up with a plan. Wiesbaden has low-income housing for seniors. She has a green card, but never gave up her German citizenship. She will talk to the manager of her sister's retirement place and see what it might cost to rent an apartment of her own.

After the takeoff, food comes. The lettuce has brown edges and she doesn't eat it. Ravioli is a treat and the buttered roll tastes good. She must sleep on the flight and fortify herself for what awaits her on the other end: the emotion of the reunion with her sister and the angst she feels in the presence of large and noisy groups, where her single hearing aid makes it impossible to pluck out a strand of conversation. Through the thin wall behind her seat, she can certainly hear the toilet well enough. Each flush sounds like a waterfall.

With the trays down, she can't reach her purse. She wraps her hearing aid in a napkin and brushes cake crumbs from her blouse. The flight attendant pushes the food cart down the aisle, and just as she would at home, Klara stacks cups and wads up wrappers. The flight attendant removes the leftovers. Klara folds her arms and settles back, only to feel the emptiness of her hand. The seat belt sign comes on, and when she looks toward the galley, the stewardesses have buckled themselves in. Her arm is too short to reach the call button. By the time the seat belt sign goes off, the cabin lights have dimmed. She cannot really ask a Lufthansa stewardess in her tailored uniform to bend over a garbage can, and Klara is dismayed that, again, a hearing aid has disappeared. Just to be sure, she pats her chest, feels in the folds of her skirt, and searches the seat pocket.

This time, she knows exactly what happened. She should have worn a cardigan. But wait. Losing a hearing aid is not the end of the world. It is only a piece of equipment. Money, yes, but not irreplaceable. They sell hearing aids in Germany. Better ones, probably. Her niece Gisela will know where to find them, and if Klara can get them ordered tomorrow or the day after, then surely, they will arrive in time for the party. Her sister's children and grandchildren. One or two old neighbors, those still around.

Hours later, the plane bumps down through a thunderstorm, and Klara sees the businessman in the window seat cross himself and bend over his knees. She could be that flexible if she were lying on the floor, but her joints are stiff, she has retained water, and her shoes are very tight. It takes ages to pry herself out of the seat. She manages passport control on her own, handing her book to the agent for a stamp, and enters a large, silent hall, full of horseshoe-shaped conveyor belts. The police dogs with their sharp ears and alert black eyes make her nervous, and she thinks of a long-ago trip to Berlin where men looked under the car with mirrors. Thankfully, a porter is there to lift the suitcase in which she has packed everything she will need for an indefinite stay. The rollers make the bag feel almost light.

When the aluminum doors swing open to let the arrivals through, she sees beaming welcomers, a hubbub if she could only hear it, look past her for the people they came to meet. Touching her newly empty ear, she searches the faces. Nowhere is there anyone she recognizes.

SHE SITS AT a coffee place and stirs the bitter grounds with a tiny spoon. She's used to American coffee, the Dunkin' Donuts brand Rolf brings her from CVS. Gisela must be delayed by bad weather or an accident on the *autobahn*. Here she is, sitting in Frankfurt, no way to call her niece unless she takes out a piece of paper, writes down a message, and asks someone else to make the call. Meanwhile, since she has time on her hands, she can review her options one more time. See if there is something she has missed.

Gisela, her niece, is well off and has a large house, but, even so, she let Zelda go to a home. Asking Gisela is not an option. Klara wishes Rolf would take her in. This would have been the simplest plan. Let Klara occupy the small bedroom that has its own bath and a door to the patio. He won't though. He doesn't want trouble with his wife. Forty years ago, Klara could have made that better. Too late now.

Her hands begin to shake. For the first time in years she wishes she had a cigarette. She can't believe Marlies has started up with that nasty habit again.

A waiter comes by and she orders another coffee, pointing to the cup because she can't hear him. Gisela should have been waiting at international arrivals. Klara has come all this way.

On the good side, she has her suitcase. She has her passport. She has her German money, two hundred fifty Deutschemarks, which she has saved since her last trip in 1998. Five hundred dollars in travelers' checks should be enough. They are old, too.

She looks toward a family of Turkish guest workers, the women in head scarves and ankle-length coats, children in strollers, sallow-faced men in sport coats and tweed hats, the kind newsboys used to wear. She has forgotten what a crowded place the world is, and, parked here in this sea of bodies, she feels adrift. If she can just get to Zelda, she will be able to put down an anchor and figure out how to move ahead.

Zelda. Happy, carefree twin. There's a picture in her mind of the two of them skipping down a cobbled street, hands linked, singing "Lustig Ist Das Zigeunerleben," the gypsy's life is free and fun. Closing her eyes, rocking slightly, she hugs herself and hums a few bars, putting herself back in her young body and feeling the clasp of Zelda's hand.

Water splatters Klara's face. She opens her eyes. Gisela is shaking a wet umbrella. A plastic rain hat accordions over her hair. She has on a shiny, black poncho that drips.

"Are you completely mad? I've looked for you everywhere." Gisela bends down so her face is inches away. "Didn't you hear the service announcement over the loudspeaker?"

Klara turns her ear. "I lost my hearing aids."

"We don't have time to look for them."

"It's not necessary. I will buy new ones."

"Don't you have some old ones you can put in?"

"No, those were my only pair."

Gisela looks down the line of brightly lit shops. Shaking her head, she takes Klara by the elbow and pulls her to her feet.

"Let me go!" Klara clamps her elbow to her side. "I can walk unassisted."

"Really?" Gisela looks Klara up and down. "Come on, then.

I'm in short term parking."

"I haven't given them money for my coffee." Klara unfolds her Deutschemarks.

"No, no." Gisela wags her finger. "We're using euros now."

"Can I change these at a bank?" Klara asks.

"Only at Deutsche Bank," Gisela says.

"I have travelers' checks."

"No one takes those."

Gisela intercepts the waiter, pays, and links elbows. On the way to the car, Klara slows down, a form of resistance she has perfected at home. The car door doesn't need a key to open. Gisela punches in a code, and, by now, Klara is glad to sit. The leather interior smells like a new purse, not like Marlies's Tercel, which reeks of stale smoke and cold French fries. On the highway, rain splashes up from the road, sending sheets of water against the windshield. Finally getting around to apologizing for arriving late, her niece drives ten feet from the taillights of the car ahead, as if the two were attached by an imaginary rope. Klara hopes the car has an air bag, but it probably does since it's a BMW.

ZELDA'S RETIREMENT CENTER looks just like the pictures, a three-story, brick building with a portico. The car idles at the curb, and Gisela helps Klara get out. The rain is horizontal, but the portico shields her from the worst of it.

"Now wait here while I park," Gisela shouts. She goes around to the driver's side and calls over the top, "The sidewalk is slippery. Don't fall."

There is a command buried in her niece's instructions, an "I dare you to disobey me" tone. Gisela is almost like a daughter. A few years back — Or can it be decades? — Gisela loved to shop at Gurnee Mills, the large outlet mall near Chicago. However, if there is one thing Klara has learned and tried to reconcile herself to, it's that there's a reversal going on. She can't say just when it happened, but her children and niece have begun to treat her like a stubborn child. She must remember to be gracious.

With the poncho held over her head, Gisela splashes through puddles and hops up on the curb. "I promised Mutti I would get you here by two, and I don't want to disappoint."

Klara expects her sister to be waiting in the lobby, but she is not. Upstairs on the third floor, a woman in a light blue tunic leads Klara to a handrail that runs the length of the corridor. As soon as the nurse turns her back, Klara lets go. She wants to see Zelda's face, which, after all, is her own face, and she needs to convince her sister to get up — Stand up! — not let herself be "stabilized" here. The place is clean enough, but not the way Klara had pictured it. The corridor is linoleum and in the glare of floor wax, Klara sees wheel marks. A cloying, lemon scent makes her take shallow breaths. Blood pools in her ankles. At the end of the corridor, the sign for the fire exit glows red. The stairs must have a handrail. Given enough time, she could make it outdoors. But, then, the rain.

Her niece pushes open a wide, maple door. It is a hospital room with a hospital bed. Like a highchair's plastic tray, the headboard and footboard have a molded edge, as if to keep a baby from pushing peas on the floor.

Gisela lowers the guardrail and brings a chair for Klara to sit. A small brush with yellow bristles lies on the nightstand. Trailing from the bristles are long white hairs.

When she can bring herself to look at the woman lying with her head in the pillow's dip, she sees a familiar widow's peak. Her sister's eyebrows have all but disappeared, replaced by shiny S-curves. Like Hessenstickerei, wrinkles stitch and pucker her skin.

Klara leans over and says in German, "How are you?"

"Not good." The words rattle up from Zelda's chest.

Somewhere inside this body, shrunken on the bed, her sister still exists. On the coverlet a hand crabs toward Klara's knee. Touching it is like touching a limp and clammy rubber glove.

Her sister's lips move.

Klara lowers an ear.

"Do you still feel nineteen?" Zelda asks.

Spittle hits Klara's cheek. She wipes it off. "Not today."

Her sister's breath smells like rancid bacon. White whiskers sprout from Zelda's chin. Once, as girls riding on tanks, they'd gotten cigarettes from GIs. Nylons and chocolate, too. Klara, scarcely believing that they can never return to their young lives, straightens up.

GISELA'S CAR WITH its black-tinted windows swings around the parking lot. Klara stands with her back to the rain. Her handkerchief is full of tears and snot, and if she uses it to clean her lenses, she'll be blind as well as deaf.

Letting the engine idle, Gisela trots around the car and opens the passenger door. She lifts Klara's knees and helps her swivel around. Then Gisela grabs the seat belt and buckles it. Leaning in the open door and speaking loudly in Klara's ear, her niece says, "It must be hard for you, seeing her like that."

"True," Klara says. Almost unendurable. "Her body is failing all at once."

"She has been hanging on till you got here."

"Hanging by a thread."

"We will come again tomorrow," Gisela says.

"What about the party?" Klara says.

"Under the circumstances," Gisela says, "I think we will bring a small cake to her room."

"I hope the candles don't set off a fire alarm."

"What?" Gisela says.

"Ninety candles."

"Oh, don't worry," Gisela says. "The cake won't have that many. You'd never be able to blow them out."

"How many will there be?"

"Two, I think, or possibly one."

One. So maybe a birthday and a funeral.

The door slams, leaving Klara alone in the leather-smelling car. Tomorrow, she must ask Gisela for help getting new hearing aids, and she must go to the bank and change her worthless currency. With that, and if it's not too much trouble for her niece to rebook the ticket, Klara would like to go home earlier than she'd planned.

A MESSAGE FROM THE AUTHOR

———○———

T HANK YOU FOR reading *Body Language*. I hope you
enjoyed meeting John and Sally, Olympia, Arlo, Porter,
Sunny, Salina, Neva and Otto, Klara and the spelunkers in the
Spanish cave. If you did, I would greatly appreciate you leaving
a review on the review site of your choice. Reviews are crucial
for any author, and a line or two about your experience can make
a huge difference. If you're part of the Goodreads' community,
comments there are especially valuable.

www.goodreads.com

What's up next? My next book is *Surrender: A Memoir*.

1961. High school sweethearts. An unplanned pregnancy.
Lives changed in an instant.

Surrender is the touching story of an adult's search for iden-
tity and the healing power of a mother's love.

Learn more about this book and others on my website:

www.maryleemacdonald.com

ACKNOWLEDGMENTS

THANK YOU TO everyone who helped make these stories a reality. My husband, Bruce Rittmann, is my first reader and unfailingly makes me believe that writing is a worthwhile endeavor. I'm also grateful that my children and grandchildren listen patiently when I yammer on about my imaginary friends.

Members of my writing groups in Phoenix and Evanston have also played a big part in helping me shape the clay of my rough drafts. Special thanks in that regard go to my writing colleagues, Greg Williams and Chandra Graham Garcia, and to my long-distance developmental editor, Kathy Hughes, all three of whom seem to intuit what it is I mean to say and then tactfully find ways to help me polish the prose. And, to my beta readers, I can't praise you enough. No matter how carefully I go over a manuscript, there are always typos. I'm grateful to you for finding them and saving me from embarrassment.

I'm also grateful to literary magazines that have made room in their pages for these stories, many of which are longer than stories such magazines typically publish. A complete list of these can be found on the copyright page.

One final thanks to my cover designer. Maurizio Marotta's beautiful images inspire me to polish my stories to a high shine.

ABOUT THE AUTHOR

———◦———

BEFORE TURNING TO fiction, Marylee MacDonald worked as a carpenter and magazine editor. Her nonfiction has appeared in *Sunset, Better Homes & Gardens*, and the *Old-House Journal*. She holds a Master's in English/Creative Writing from San Francisco State, and her short stories have won the Barry Hannah Prize, the Jeanne M. Leiby Memorial Chapbook Award, the *American Literary Review Fiction Prize*, the Ron Rash Award, the *Seven Hills* fiction contest, and *New Delta Review's* Matt Clark Prize.

Her debut novel, *Montpelier Tomorrow*, won a Gold Medal for Drama from Readers' Favorites International Book Awards, and her short story collection, *Bonds of Love & Blood*, was a *Foreword Reviews* INDIEFab Finalist.

When she's not writing, she's walking on a beach, strolling in a redwood forest, plucking snails from her tomatoes, or hiking in the red rocks of Sedona.

BOOK CLUB QUESTIONS

———○———

1. In "Long Time, No See," Tom gets roped into becoming a caregiver. Do you have relatives who are "outliers," but who still need a relative to step in?

2. What does Olympia's conversation with the bartender reveal about her deeper hungers? Is it only hot cocoa she wants, or is that a substitute for a deeper craving?

3. Which stories felt the most tense? Did the tension arise from the characters' actions or from their internal struggles?

4. In "Ink" and "All I Have," did you see any notable racial or cultural factors at play? What images or sensory information contributed to the main characters' fears?

5. "Tito's Descent" is a story about a single event that shaped a woman's outlook on life. Is there a single event that shaped your life or the life of another family member?

6. It is said that a short story is a slice of life, whereas a novel represents a whole life. What do you imagine will happen to Klara when she returns to Chicago?

7. Neva needed to get back to composing. Was her interest in Otto ever going to lead to a relationship, or was Otto, and the commission he offered, a means to what would ultimately bring her greater happiness?

8. Why did John tell himself it was okay for him to cheat on his wife? Was his decision to go fishing with Sally anything more than a long-deferred, teenage infatuation?

9. How did Amelia's story about the mongoose help Gwen "reframe" her picture of her father and of herself?

10. How did Salina Limone's childhood poverty shape her personality?

11. In "The Memory Palace" the author gives us access to the bartender's thoughts and his struggle with sobriety. By the end of the story, can you see a ray of hope that he is strong enough to resist temptation?

12. What was your experience reading a series of short stories compared to the experience of reading a novel? Were you glad to finish a story and then find yourself in a different world, or did it take time to make the transition?

MONTPELIER TOMORROW

(Excerpt from the novel)

————○————

TIME ROBS US of chances for reconciliation. Time makes us liars. I wanted to save my daughter, and even now, I don't know what made me think I could keep her from going through what I had gone through, widowed and pregnant, all at the same time. The scars from her father's death had never fully healed, but if not for Tony's illness, Sandy would have sailed into her future and I would have gone on trying to save the world, one kindergartner at a time.

That June, when I closed up my classroom and headed off to Washington, D.C., I teetered on the brink of an exciting transition. For the past few years, aging parents had kept me in Chicago. Not that I begrudged them: This was the natural progression of a woman's life, or so it seemed, even though women of my generation thought we had liberated ourselves from traditional roles. You can't really free yourself from love though, nor from the surprise that middle-age doesn't mean you have more time for yourself. Children leave the nest about the time parents grow frail. One minute you're changing babies' diapers and the next you're tugging up Depends.

My mother had died. I missed her terribly, but her death had freed me. Finally, with an unencumbered heart, I could see my daughter's new house and help when the second grandchild arrived. The birth would give me a chance to make amends for the baby showers and birthdays I had missed.

Standing on the sidewalk in Glover Park, a neighborhood in the capital's northwest quadrant, I looked from my day-timer to the rusted numbers above a set of tilted concrete steps. In the upstairs windows, the blinds had yellowed. Brown paint, like shaved chocolate, curled back from the porch-beams. Next to the door, plastic recycling bins overflowed with newsprint. The grass looked brittle and the azaleas dead. Hoping I'd written down the wrong address and ignoring the clues that something disastrous might be wrong, I prepared a smile I might have brought with a casserole or condolence flowers.

An envelope poked from the mail slot. Surreptitiously, I slid it out. A letter for Tony Dimasio. Yep, I had the right address. Tony, my son-in-law, was a good-looking punster with scads of friends—lacrosse friends, college and law school buddies, environmental activists, reporters—and he had pursued Sandy as if she were the hottest babe on the planet. Which to him, she was. Her savings had paid for their first house.

Sighing at the mountain of work that awaited them, I cupped my hand against the glare and pressed my nose to the door's glass panel. Sandy had no idea what it really took to fix up a place, even though she had seen me do it a dozen times, and I feared she'd taken on too much. Before I could even catch a glimpse of the interior, the clomp of footsteps made me back away.

Sandy's face appeared. A nutmeg of summer freckles. A smile. The door flew open. "Mom!"

Like her father, Sandy had deep-set eyes. In bright light, they looked blue, but in the shadows of the porch, her eyes reminded me of clouds before a storm. In the years since her teenage rebellion had come at me like projectile vomit, I'd learned to watch for the early warning signs of her bad moods. I saw none now. Since Christmas, her belly had inflated to the size of my exercise ball. She was nine months pregnant and the baby had dropped. A flowered jumper hung from her bare, hunched shoulders. Sandy had never been much of a hugger, but this time she threw her arms around me, a drowning person lunging for the life preserver. Which was my neck.

"Don't choke me," I said, disentangling her arms.

"Thank God you're here," she said.

Reflexively, I tucked in her bra strap. "I can't believe the pregnancy's almost done."

Sandy looked sideways at my hand, and then brushed it aside to massage her shoulder. "I hate my bony arms. Even eating for two, I can't seem to put on weight."

"You look fabulous, honey."

"I must look better than I feel," Sandy said. A taut grin flipped up like a mask. "Well, you're here, at least, but I expected you an hour ago."

Maybe we could rewind this to the knock. Had I said something or done something to deserve this tiny flash of anger? I'd tucked in her strap. That was it, and I should have known not to. She could not stand to be touched or drawn into an embrace. At that moment, however, her brief hug had left me wanting more: a longer and less desperate hug, the downy softness of her cheek against mine, or a map crumpled to bring Chicago and Washington, D.C. closer together.

"I really should have pulled over and called you," I said, still searching for what had made her say she hated her bony arms and why she was angry because I had arrived an hour late. "I thought about calling, but then I thought it'd just make me later and anyway, I had a map so I wasn't lost, just playing pin the tail on the donkey."

Exhaling, she reared back.

"Sandy, please," I said. "I came to help, not get in your way."

She must have had a long day, but so had I. Weary from the drive and the demands of the last few months, I needed a refuge. "Can I come in?"

"Sure. I don't know why we're standing outside in this heat." Backing into the living room she looked around. "The place is a pigsty, but, oh well, you can't do everything."

The inside looked better than the exterior. No books on the end tables, no out-of-place couch cushions, and, surprisingly, no toys on the floor.

"The place is definitely not a pigsty," I said.

She shook her head. "I try to keep it picked up, but it's hard because Josh doesn't have a playroom. We have a basement, but it's so dingy I can hardly bear to go down there."

She had planted a hook in my mouth. I felt the barb, but let her reel me in. "Maybe I can do a little painting while I'm here."

"Oh, would you, Mom?" Sandy said. "That would just be amazing."

"Sure," I said, though on the two-day drive out, painting Sandy's basement had been the last thing on my mind.

"I'm trying to get the house organized, baby clothes washed and in drawers, and work's crazy. Some cases I can't delegate because I'm the lead attorney." Sandy checked her watch. "Oh, no. I'm late."

I'm late, I'm late, for a very important date. "Where are you going?" I said.

"A doctor's appointment." Sandy grabbed her purse. "They're squeezing us in at the end of the day, and I didn't find out about it until a couple of hours ago. Can you watch Josh? He's upstairs in his crib."

"Sure." I followed her to the porch.

Holding her watermelon belly, she jogged to the car. Just like the White Rabbit. No time to say hello, good-bye, I'm late,

I'm late, I'm late. In the parking strip Sandy opened the car door.

"Should I wake Josh at a certain time?" I called.

"Let him sleep. His teacher said he didn't nap."

"How long will you be gone?"

"An hour or so." Sandy slid back the seat of her Toyota Tercel. The car had scratched bumpers and a caved-in passenger door, an almost new car turning into a junker. She roared out of the parking space.

Sandy's brothers joked that she'd never learned to tell time, but that didn't matter because she had lots of other skills. She'd never find herself in my situation, *Broke, With Children*. My life would have made a good sitcom.

Back in the house I knelt on the couch and tried to raise the front windows: painted shut and no curtains. A stroller stood in the corner. I could have taken Josh out for a walk, but Sandy hadn't left a key. I opened the TV hutch. On the shelves below the boob tube sat wooden puzzles and LEGO blocks. Good for fine-motor skills.

Grabbing blunt-nosed scissors from the dining room table, I returned to the porch and eased into a plastic chair. From the recycling bin, I separated out two pages of the *Washington Post*, folding and refolding the newsprint until I held a rectangle the size of a book. The key to making paper-dolls, paper-houses, or paper anything was to start with the right shape, fold in the same direction, and leave part of the fold uncut. In my classroom, I always had something like this on the windows—leaves in fall, pumpkins in October, and snowmen at Christmas. Across the street the houses had twisted, licorice porch railings, attics with small, winking windows, and chimney pots smack in the center of tiny slate roofs. A neighborhood of Hobbit houses. And here was Sandy's. Dead azaleas and recycling bins.

Inside, I threw the paper houses on the couch. Until I could get curtains made, I'd tape up the cityscape to provide privacy.

Sandy must have tape on her desk. Upstairs, the door to the right opened to the master bedroom—the room with the yellowed shades. On Sandy's desk, next to a wicker basket of unpaid bills, sat a roll of American-flag stamps. No tape. Maybe Josh had used it up. When my kids were little, I could never find a roll of tape to save my soul. I looked at the indent in the chenille spread, the pillows propped against the wall, and a novel she'd tossed on the bed. *How Stella Got Her Groove Back.* I sniff-laughed. That book had inspired me to dip into the barrel and see if I could pull out an edible apple. I hadn't found the young hunk Stella found, only some bruised bananas.

In the room across the hall, Josh lay spread-eagled. Small for three, he had Tony's black curls and Sandy's fair skin. His pink neck felt hot to the touch. The nursery school teacher had forgotten to hit it with sun block. Three-to-six was my favorite age. They were little philosophers, as I had seen last Christmas, when Josh said he thought dolphins had a secret language and someday he would learn to speak it. The Spiderman shirt, one of my presents, had faded. An inch of skin showed above his shorts. I hated these big gaps between visits, and I hoped the creak of stairs as I descended would wake him.

The paper houses had dropped like a slinky from the couch. I should tape up the diorama before Josh needed attention, but where had Sandy put the tape? A drawer to the left of the sink held silverware, and below it, the drawer my mother always called the "Fibber McGee and Molly" drawer: string, screwdrivers, thumbtacks, birthday candles, white glue, and the odd button. Whether women wanted to or not, we took on our mother's patterns: spices in the cabinet to the left of the microwave, cookie sheets in the oven drawer. I could be blind and cook a meal here.

A pen-mug sat on the counter. Next to a stack of unopened bills sat a roll of tape. Twirling it around my finger, I whistled softly, trying to fill a silence broken only by the bark of a neighbor's dog and a motorcycle's distant cough. Kneeling on the denim couch, I taped the paper houses to the windows. The silhouette reminded me of the skyline at the Adler Planetarium. Newsprint blocked the view of parked cars, but that was good. If I couldn't see out, no one could see in. Breastfeeding Josh, Sandy had always thrown a receiving blanket over her shoulder. A private person, she wouldn't want every Tom, Dick, and Harry looking through her windows.

With no more self-assigned tasks, I thought about taking a look at the basement, but the heat punctured my balloon of good intentions. I can picture myself innocently walking through the house, curious about the life my daughter had begun to construct for herself. It was the last moment of tranquility before fate blindsided me. Blindsided me again, I should say, because my husband's death had come at me in much the same way, on a day so ordinary that such an alteration of circumstances seemed unimaginable.

The screen door wheezed open, and I stood on the porch. The rooflines' spiked shadows had advanced across the small, square lawns. Across the street, a paper skeleton hung on the door, a relic of last year's Halloween. When I heard a hubcap scrape the curb, I turned.

Their Toyota sedan was backing into a parking space. Tony sat in the passenger seat. Usually, he drove. Sandy, on the driver's side, turned off the engine. Then she leaned on the steering wheel and stared straight ahead, the way people do when they're having a fight and trying to decide whether to finish it or go in. I leaned on the porch rail, fearing that Tony had crossed her in some way. Better him than me. Finally, she opened her door. One hand at the crook of her back, the other on the hood, she went around to Tony's door and opened it. Tony started to get out but fell to his knees and curled up in a ball.

I stood. My mouth went dry. "Tony, are you all right?"

"I'm okay," he called.

"I've got him, Mom," Sandy said.

To keep myself from dashing down the stairs, I grabbed the railing and prayed that Sandy wouldn't injure herself. Holding him under the elbow, she lifted him to his feet and brushed grass from his pants. He swiped an arm across his forehead. His cheeks looked flushed. At work he glad-handed so many people he'd probably picked up a bug. When he felt better I'd tease him and ask if the halls of Congress needed an Elvis impersonator: Since Christmas, he'd grown muttonchops shaped like the boot of Italy.

Sandy unlocked the trunk and took out his sport coat. Letting her carry it and shuffling his feet, he came up the walk. I held the screen.

Inside, Tony flopped down on the sofa, the one beneath my paper silhouette. Stretched out full length, he put one foot up on the sofa's arm and left the other on the floor. His shoelace had come undone, and though tempted to kneel down and tie it, I didn't want him to feel like he'd gone back to kindergarten.

"You look like you had a terrible day," I said.

"The longest day of my life," he said.

I put my palm on his forehead. It felt clammy, not hot. He drew his hands to his chin. His chest heaved, but no sound came out. Elbowing me aside, Sandy bent over Tony and put her arms around him.

He pushed her away. "Too hot."

Sandy went to the kitchen. Water splashed. When she returned, her bangs dripped. "Where's Josh?" she said.

"Asleep," I said.

"He won't sleep tonight, but then, I guess that's all right because I won't either." Sandy sank down onto the other sofa and bumped a framed poster from the National Zoo, a mother panda with a protective paw curled around her baby. My legs shook, and I backed toward the rocking chair.

"Hey, Colleen, do you happen to have a handkerchief?" Tony said. Beads of moisture dotted his upper lip.

I always carried packages of tissue to wipe runny noses. Reaching out, I handed one over.

He blew his nose. "So, did Sandy tell you what this was all about?"

"I didn't want to worry her," Sandy said.

"What should I be worried about?"

"My finger." Tony held up the index finger of his right hand. It moved like the second-hand of a clock: tick, tick, tick. Not a smooth motion.

"What's wrong with it?" I said.

"Since March, we've been thinking he had a pinched nerve," Sandy said.

This was June. "What do you have, carpal tunnel?"

"I wish." Tony propped himself on an elbow, opened his mouth, and pointed to his tongue.

"He was testifying a month ago on Capitol Hill—" Sandy said.

"A swine farm bill was coming up—" Tony said.

"And he got so tongue-tied—"

"I couldn't speak," Tony said.

"You?" Driving through Ohio, I'd heard him interviewed on public radio. There'd been a call-in program on factory farms. The stench. The animals' living conditions. It wasn't an issue I'd ever thought twice about, but Tony had been so eloquent, I'd actually begun to think the animal-rights folks had a point.

Tony pulled up his shirt. The dark, curly hair, once thick on his chest, had been shaved clean, leaving only the stubble. Dozens of white circles the size of bottle caps dotted his chest. He looked like he'd been stood against a wall and used for dart-gun target practice.

"I saw this neurologist —"

"Two, actually," Sandy said.

"The second doctor was a mom from our nursery school," Tony said.

"She saw Sandy coming down the elevator, just losing it."

"So she brought him back upstairs and ran the tests again," Sandy said.

"I had a hundred electrodes on my body."

"Nipples and everything," Sandy said.

Tony looked down at his chest. He shuddered. "They shocked me over and over again. I felt like a rat in an experiment."

"After the second battery of nerve tests," Sandy said, "the doctor told him he has ALS."

Through the open screen came the hum of tires and the urgent ring of a tinny bell. Riding a purple bicycle with training wheels, a curly-headed girl, biting her tongue, stood on the pedals. Her mother jogged behind, close enough to grab the seat. The ring echoed long after they'd passed.

Tony pulled down his shirt. "The doc said I have Lou Gehrig's Disease." He shook his head from side to side, moaned, and put a hand over his eyes and the other on his heart. "I thought I had it right from the start. I mean, that was what the HMO doc told me back in March, that I had ALS, and I thought if I did, I could be brave and suck it up, but it's different when neurologists tell you for sure."

Sandy reached over and massaged Tony's foot and with her other hand pressed her belly. "The baby's quiet."

"Probably sleeping," I said. One domino-disaster tipping another. That's what she feared.

Tony blew his nose and wiped his eyes with a corner of his shirt. "I'd better start dinner."

"You can't be in a mood to cook," I said. "Let's order pizza."

Tony stood up. "I have stuff for spaghetti."

I followed him to the kitchen. The doctors had to be wrong. Tony was in the prime of life, a lacrosse player, a runner, and lately, a vegetarian. He took an onion from the refrigerator. After peeling off the dry outer layers, he used the flat of his hand to force down the blade.

"After Christmas, when Sandy saw her brothers in the kitchen, she said I had to learn to cook. I actually like it, and I want to cook while I can."

"While you can . . ." I wanted to draw out this moment, the moment when I couldn't yet see around the corner. "Can what?"

"Cook, of course." Tony stared at me. "My muscles will atrophy."

"I don't know much about ALS."

"Actually, I don't either," Tony said, "except I've got it."

Trying to have a normal conversation and accept this news as if Tony were telling me about a raise or a promotion, I found myself increasingly upset. I thought of the Chinese woman who lived two doors down from my new house and how she'd stand on the porch in the bitterest weather, going through her *tai chi* exercises. Balance in slow motion. I opened the silverware drawer and took out knives and forks.

"What, exactly, did the doctor say?"

"A lot of men get it."

"So what are they going to do?"

"Nothing they can do," he said.

"Nothing?" I said. "But there's something they can do for everything."

He shook his head like it was a fait accompli and dumped onions in a cast-iron skillet, one that had belonged to my mother. I wondered how I could possibly deal with this loss when I'd barely absorbed her death, and immediately felt ashamed that the first thought that bubbled up was whether I had space inside my skin for another grief this big. This was Sandy's tragedy, not mine.

"Have you got another kleenex?" Sandy called from the living room

"She can have this." Tony handed me the rest of the packet.

I took it, returned to the living room, and sat down next to Sandy, who leaned against me. Like a kitten on a tree, she dug her nails into my shoulders. Tears soaked my blouse.

"Your daughter's upset," Tony called from the kitchen.

"I can see that."

On the second floor the toilet flushed.

Sandy lifted her head. "Josh is awake." She blew her nose and crumpled the kleenex in her fist.

"Do you want me to throw that away?" I said.

Sandy held out the damp wad. "My body feels all numb, like it went to the body dentist."

Mine did, too. "Where's your trash?"

"Under the sink."

"Sandy, could you open this can?" Tony said.

Letting out a silent scream, Sandy flung her head back, bumping the panda poster.

I leapt up. "Let me help him."

"Thanks so much, Mom. I've had Braxton-Hicks all day."

"I've heard the word, but what is it?"

"Contractions," Sandy said.

"But they stop if she sits," Tony said.

"In my day, we called that going into labor."

Sandy put her hands on her stomach. "I don't think it's true labor. I hope not, anyway. My due date's not for another ten days."

"Mom," a little voice called from upstairs. I helped Sandy to her feet, but I had to lean back and counterbalance her weight, or she would have pulled me down.

"I'm coming," Sandy said.

The voice said, "I need you to wipe me."

"Could someone open this can?" Tony said.

I went into the kitchen. "What do you need?"

A can of pomodoro tomatoes sat on the counter. Tony held out a can opener. "My fingers don't have the strength."

I picked up the tomatoes and squeezed the can opener's handles. Air hissed.

"One thing I don't quite get," I said, "is what happens. I mean, what's the progression of the disease?"

"I have a year to live," Tony said. "Maybe less."

"No way!" The can dropped on the counter. The lid sprang open. "Are you sure?"

"I'm just going by what the doctor said." Tears streaming, he looked over his shoulder. "Fifty-five's the average age."

"But you're only thirty-four."

"I was young, she said."

I put my arms around him, but he pushed me away. "I need to finish dinner."

Tony broke spaghetti into the pot, stirring the pasta with a wooden spoon. He wiped his forehead with the back of his arm. "Shit, it's hot," he said.

"That's because the back side of the house faces east, and you're getting the late afternoon sun."

"Sandy said you'd have known that and not let us buy it. It's the one thing about the house she hates."

"Unless I'd come by at the end of the day, I wouldn't have flagged that as a problem. I told her to hire a home inspector."

"Well, she's over it so you can relax."

"Over what?"

"Over being angry because you didn't fly out."

Eyes down, I laid out silverware and napkins. "My mother

was dying."

"Yeah, well. Sandy needed you and you didn't come."

"A home inspector looks at homes full time. Most of them are engineers or former contractors. I doubt I could have told her anything more than what they wrote up in their report."

"You don't have to sound so defensive," he said.

"But … oh, never mind," I said.

The last three weeks of mother's life had passed in a blur. I had to make decisions about a feeding tube or comfort measures. Sips of water dwindled down to ice chips and spongy swabs of her tongue. I couldn't reconstruct when exactly, in that blur of days, Sandy had called. And, of course, my daughter had a right to feel let down. No one could understand what the inversion of roles meant, the child behaving as a parent, making end-of-life decisions for an emaciated, vacant-minded shell. Sandy had just started her journey. The first house. The second baby. And now this.

Tony bit into a noodle. "*Al dente.*" He looked at me. "Whole wheat. The noodles turn mushy if you cook them too long."

Tony. The newbie in the kitchen. My boys would have found his sudden culinary interest hilarious. But then, no they wouldn't. Not now.

Sandy came down holding Josh by the hand. Smiling, she looked down at her son. "Do you remember Grandma?"

"You're Mommy's mommy." Josh's eyebrows looked like charcoal smudges and from beneath them shone two blue marbles. Rob's eyes and the eyes of Sandy's brothers.

"Remember last Christmas we went to an aquarium where they had dolphins?" I said.

"And jellyfish." Josh tugged his mother's hand.

She smiled.

"It's time for dinner, Josh," Tony said. "Get the stepstool and wash your hands."

"He washed upstairs," Sandy said.

"Could somebody dump the water out of the pan and put the sauce on the noodles?" Tony said.

I did as he asked and put food on the table. Josh climbed into his booster seat and buckled the strap.

"No salad?" Sandy said.

"I'm not in the mood," Tony said.

"I don't like tomato sauce," Josh said.

I wondered if the opening gambit of this negotiation were for my benefit or if they negotiated every meal. That kind of thing wore me out.

"Daddy made a nice dinner," I said. "Why don't you try one bite?"

"I already know I won't like it," Josh said. "It's red."

"He likes plain noodles with butter and cheese." Sandy went into the kitchen and rummaged in the refrigerator. She put a turkey roll on his plate. "He's fine with this."

I twirled my spaghetti. The sauce tasted burnt. Maybe I could bargain for a turkey roll.

"What's wrong?" Tony said, his dark eyes glaring at me from across the table. "Don't you like it, either?"

In my stomach, a gerbil raced madly on a wheel. "No, it's fine. Whole grain noodles. Very nutritious."

Standing behind Josh's chair, Sandy took a taste of spaghetti, frowned, and put her plate down on the counter, a pass-through between the narrow dining room and aisle kitchen. "The humidity takes away my appetite."

Tony looked up at her. He hadn't touched his dinner. We were pretending to be normal for as long as we could.

"Why don't you take Josh outside and let me do the dishes?" I said.

"I guess we could do that," Sandy said. "It's still light."

"Okay," Tony said. "Fresh air would feel good."

I cleared the dishes, listening to the tape that ran in my head whenever I wasted food. Think of the starving children in Armenia. The distant tragedy flashed up from my childhood, and it was the rare meal that found me leaving a bite of food on my plate. The spaghetti was really, really bad. I dumped it into the garbage.

On the dead grass that passed for a lawn, Sandy found a wiffle ball.

Tony wrapped his arms around Josh's shoulders, showing him how to swing a plastic bat. Josh connected. The ball bounced across two neighbors' lawns into a clump of ice plant. He gave a whoop, then raced, his arms pumping. All elbows and knobby knees, he looked like a cricket.

"Did you see that one?" Josh held up the ball. "Wasn't that a great one?"

"That was good, Josh." Tony looked over at me, sitting on the porch.

"I always dreamed of taking my kids to Yankees' games. Josh won't remember this."

I leaned over the railing. "Why don't I take Josh to the park and give you some time to decompress?"

"No, that's okay," Sandy said.

Tony wiped his brow. His face turned sullen and Sandy looked at him.

"Then again," Sandy said, "maybe that's a good idea."

To read what happens next, buy *Montpelier Tomorrow* at your favorite bookstore today.

Made in the USA
Monee, IL
26 March 2020